G000067105

Contents

Chapter 1

Faylan had dreaded this day for the last 70 years of her life. She was to meet the man she was meant to marry. Her mother had only said, "he's a respectable man my love, nothing to be worried about." This made Faylan snort "That's easy for you to say, you're not going through it, you knew Father before you married him." This comment made her mother chuckle, Faylan was right of course. Her mother and father had met almost 3 centuries ago when the families of Rohana and Admaris came together to fight the ogres. Faylan had heard the story of how her mother had made the joke 'If we win this fight, you have to ask me to marry you." Her father had chuckled and agreed and after they'd completely obliterated the ogres, wiping them off the face of the earth, he had got down on one knee and asked her to marry him. There had never been a wedding like it, nor had there been one since. That was until now, this wedding was meant to be the wedding of the century, not that Faylan agreed with that idea. She wanted to marry for love, not because she was being forced to because it was part of being a princess.

She had been thinking about this for too long as her mother nudged her "Are you listening to me?" She asked, raising a perfect eyebrow at her. Faylan just looked confused and her mother sighed, exasperated by her lack of interest in what was going on "I said, the Acherons will be here at 30 past the 14th hour tomorrow and you need to make yourself look presentable"

"Why though? Why do I have to marry him? Why can't I marry for love, not some Vampire I've never met? That's another thing, why suddenly the mixture of species, why not another elf?" Faylan asked, crossing her slender arms across her chest and her mother groaned "It was so much better when you couldn't question our decisions" She sighed "Taeral never questioned us" she said, the bitterness and grief in her voice. Taeral was Faylan's older twin brother, he had died when they were only 20 years old, murdered by a Lycan. Faylan had been compared to him ever since, she always felt as though she was lesser than he was, and it just made the pain of his death even more unbearable. As his twin, she felt his death, even from her reading room in the palace, she had doubled over in pain, screaming her head off and sobbing. After his funeral, she had gone mute for almost 50 years and confined herself to her chambers, not wanting to experience life without him. Now she growled and spun around to face her mother, her long white hair whipping around, her porcelain face cracking with anger "I am so sorry I am not like him Mother, I am so sorry I am not as good as he was, as obedient as he was, sorry I want free will and a life of my own!" She almost shouted, her mother's face going white as Faylan stormed out of the room, her usually light feet now heavy with her wrath.

She made her way down to the Fountain of the Moon, it was her favourite place to go whenever she felt alone or sad, Taeral and her would always play in the waters when they were children with their father keeping a watchful eye from his perch on the balcony. She sat down on the white stone, watching the crystal-clear waters flow and the multi-coloured fish swim. She held back tears as she remembered all the happy times she had here with her twin. Why didn't her parents love her the same way they did him? Was it because she was a woman? Curse whatever God made her a woman and curse Taeral for dying. This whole mess could have been avoided for much longer had he still been around. No matter how hard she tried, she was never good enough for them, in combat, intellect, and obedience. All she wanted was for her life to be her own, was that too much to ask? Apparently.

She looked out at her home, from the white marble walls of the palace to the lakes teeming with all manners of creatures from fish to eels to dolphins, she looked to the forest, thinking of all that lived there, the unicorns, the two antlered deer, the bears that were the same size as the highest peak of the palace and the trees, stretching up to the sky like walls around the palace, the same size as a giant sat on the shoulders of another. The world she lived in was truly a spectacle to behold, it was no wonder that people from all over would come just to bask in its beauty.

As dinner approached, her father came down to find her "Faylan? Come inside please" he said, placing a hand on her shoulder. Her father had always been kind to her, loving. She turned to look up at him, her bright blue eyes ringed in red, her cheeks damp with tears "Why? So, I can be insulted again by Mother? I don't think so, I'd rather go hungry" she grumbled, turning back to the water as her father sighed "please my love" his voice pained and quiet, making her turn around "fine, but only because you asked nicely" she replied, making her way with him back inside to the dining hall, ignoring her mother as she sat down to what she expected to be an awkward and long dinner.

Back in her room, she sighed, it was her last night of freedom before she was to be married and shipped off to some far-off place that was unfamiliar to her. She sat in her big armchair, picking up her book, trying her best to focus on it but after a long while of her mind being elsewhere, she tossed the book aside and looked out the window at the stars, they always calmed her down when she was anxious. She loved how they glistened and twinkled in the sky, how, on a rare occasion, she could see shooting stars fly past. Taeral and her would always make wishes whenever they saw one, a childish hope that one would come true. She remembered one instance when she asked for a dragon, her brother laughed and said "Come on Fay, you know dragons don't come round here, we're too pure for them." He'd winked playfully at her, lessening the upset she'd felt. Now she saw one crossing the sky and wished, more like prayed, that she didn't have to marry, that she could marry for love and not for strategy. She spent so long looking at the stars that she didn't notice she was falling asleep, curled up in her armchair with a blanket laid across her.

~~~~~

She was awoken by her mother storming into her room, throwing the blanket off her "Come on, time to get up, you have a big day ahead of you and I need to get you looking respectable for the Acheron's arrival." she said, going through her closet and finding her best dress. Faylan sighed, getting up "Can I at least bathe in privacy?" she shot back, grabbing some towels as her mother nodded "Fine but meet me downstairs in an hour." she put the shoes she was holding down and left the room. Faylan sighed deeply, running the water for a bath, dreading the day ahead, she hated formal occasions, especially ones surrounding her. The water felt like a blanket of calm against her skin as she lay in the bathtub, taking in the scent of her lavender body wash and shampoo as she got herself ready for the day ahead. She looked at the dress her mother had chosen, it was a knee-length light blue silk dress with blue shoes to match. She put them on, looking at herself in the mirror, she was quite small for her kind, the dress hugged her curves, accentuating her figure and her cleavage so no wonder her mother chose it. She did her hair in its usual half-up half-down ponytail with tiny braids at the sides.

She made her way down the elegant, marble staircase, ignoring all the stares she was getting, her mother and father meeting her at the bottom. She took her father's arm as they walked to the throne room. She sat on her throne; it was made of the same white marble as the palace and it had ivy wound around it. Her mother and father sat on their thrones and their crowns were placed on all their heads as the main doors opened "The Acherons' are here my lord." the guard said and Faylan watched as they entered, her heart pounding so hard she thought it might explode out of her chest. 'Oh my god.' She thought as she saw him...the man she was to marry...Nikolas Acheron.

Chapter 2

Nikolas was tall, not quite as tall as an elf but still about 5'11, with long dark hair and beautiful green eyes. He was definitely nice on the eyes but Faylan couldn't quite oversee the fact that she was being married to him and she didn't know anything about him apart from what he looked like and what species he was, a vampire. The vampires were a formidable species, immortal and beautiful. They were known to be charismatic, lethal, and fiercely protective of those they cared for. They were very good politicians, having been around for so many centuries, so they knew when a match was a good one, and apparently the marriage of Faylan and Nikolas was a good one. She hated it and she could tell that he wasn't a fan of the idea either. He stood up straight but still looked as though he was being forced to be there, his mother holding his arm a little tightly as if to keep him standing straight. As they walked towards Faylan and her parents, her heart started to pound faster, her palms sweating as she rested them on her lap "Your Highness" Lady Acheron said as they got to the steps, bowing shortly, her husband and Nikolas doing the same. The king bowed his head a little "Acherons, welcome to the Elven Court."

"Thank you, my lord, your domain is just as beautiful as the tales." Lady Acheron smiled, her fangs came into view as her lips parted "My son, Nikolas." She gestured to him and he moved forward, bowing shortly, a mumble of your highness could be heard as he did so, his eyes making contact with Faylans', his mother's eyes followed his "Princess Faylan, I presume." She smiled and gave a short bow. Faylan nodded and bowed her head a little "Yes, I am, the one being forced to marry." She grumbled and her mother gave her a stern look "Faylan!"

"It's quite alright your majesty." Lady Acheron chuckled "I understand her reservations and annoyance, my son has felt the same way. If we may, we can discuss this matter elsewhere while they get acquainted?" she suggested and the king nodded, leading his wife and the Acherons into another room and Faylan looked at Nikolas, the air thick with awkwardness and anxiety. She smiled a little at him and he returned it as she stood up, completely unsure of what to do now that it was just them. Nikolas looked at her "You don't want to do this either, do you?" He said, his voice deep and smooth, his accent strange, unlike anything she'd heard before. This was her first time meeting vampires; she had met almost every other species in her long life. She shook her head

"Not really, no, I don't understand this tradition, it's outdated and completely absurd." She said and Nikolas chuckled "You have a point there, there's a girl back home that I want to marry but my parents aren't allowing it, hence why we're in this situation." He sighed and Faylan's' heart twisted a little for him, she couldn't imagine the pain of loving someone but being forced to marry someone else because of some stupid custom. "I'm sorry you have to go through that." she said, genuinely, giving him, a sad look and he shook his head "It's alright your Highness, family has to come first sometimes, even if it breaks your heart." He said dutifully, it made Faylan want to shiver, she could never be so devoted to her family, not at the expense of her own happiness. She looked down, feeling a little ashamed that she allowed herself to think like that but she couldn't help it, she loved all Elvish traditions but this one, she hated.

She jumped a little when the door swung open with force, a woman running in "I am so sorry to disturb you your Highness but I need an audience with the king." She was tall, dark-haired, and dressed very oddly for a woman, she was in black leather trousers and a red jacket, and the shirt underneath it was black. Faylan's parents would be severely disappointed in her if she showed up dressed like that but something about this woman tugged at her mind, she was stunning with her olive skin and bright red eyes. Those kinds of eyes were only earned by a witch. They always started off with normal eye colours, blue or green, or brown but once they completed their training and chose a specific type of magic, their eyes changed colours. You could tell what type of witch you were dealing with by the colour of their eyes: Lunar witches had yellow eyes, Nocturnal witches had grey eyes, Cosmic witches had pink eyes, Elemental witches had purple eyes and Dark Arts witches had red eyes. The witch before Faylan and Nikolas was very clearly a Dark Arts witch, they were the most powerful and dangerous witches, thankfully there were very few of these witches around anymore. Faylan looked at the woman in front of them and asked "What do you need an audience with my father for?"

"That is for the king and I to discuss, if you don't mind your Highness." She said politely, giving a short bow and as she said this, the doors behind them swung open and her father came out "What's going on in here?"

"This witch demands an audience with you, father." Faylan said, gesturing to the woman in front of them. The woman came forward "My name is Eliana Creighton, my lord, I bring word of the lycans." She said, the words hitting all of them like a tonne of bricks, the lycans hadn't been heard from for half a century, why were they coming out of hiding now? What did they want? "What exactly is this information you bring me?" her father broke the stunned silence after a moment, snapping Faylan out of her thoughts, and her fears "They are gearing up for war my lord, they intend on wiping the elves out, I am not sure how this is all we could get out of the one we captured before he succumbed to our tactics." Eliana said, her beautiful eyes filled with fear but her voice stayed strong, confident. The king's eyes widened and he quickly said "Well, you must come with me, quickly, so we can talk more about this, in private." He looked at Faylan who rolled her eyes, never allowed to hear anything of war. She stood up, earning a bow from Nikolas and Eliana, looking at her as she walked out the door, Eliana gave her a playful wink as she left, leaving Faylan's stomach flipping with butterflies as she walked to the fountain again.

A few hours passed as she sat by the fountain before she heard soft footsteps behind her "You know, war isn't terribly interesting" Eliana said as she sat beside her "It's a rather horrible business."

"I know that," Faylan said "I just wish I was included; I'm meant to be queen someday and I need to know about these things so I can be prepared." She sighed, looking at the clear water "It's the one thing I hate about being a woman..."

"You feel as though you're not as important as men" Eliana interrupted and Faylan nodded "Well, where I come from, we're equals, men and women are taught the same things, and trained the same way, the only thing we differ in is which magic to specialise in." She chuckled lightly, looking at Faylan who was intently listening, amazed by the idea of men and women being equals in all walks of life, she envied it, she wanted to learn to fight, to use magic, and she knew elves possessed the ability to harness magic but she'd never been taught it, only her father and brother were. "I could teach you sometime," Eliana said, breaking her out of her thoughts "To fight I mean, maybe even a bit of magic" she smiled mischievously, her red eyes glinting in the setting sun. Faylan was ecstatic, she had never been offered such lessons before and so jumped at the chance "Yes! I'd love for you to teach me" She grinned at her and their eyes met, almost as if pulled like magnets. Faylan had no idea who this witch was but she intended on getting to know her, learning from her and about her, there was a strange feeling of fate at play as Eliana stood up and gently picked up one of her hands, placing a gentle kiss on it "until tomorrow princess" she smiled and if Faylan could have photographed it, she would have, it was the most beautiful smile she'd ever seen. She stumbled on her words as she said "Until tomorrow, Eliana." And with that, she walked away, her black hair swaying as she walked, her jacket billowing out behind her in the breeze, allowing her scent to float back to Faylan, a scent she could get drunk on. She looked forward to tomorrow and whatever it had in store for her as long as Eliana was a part of it.

Chapter 3

The king woke her out of her sweet dreams of Eliana by thrusting open the curtains and sitting beside her on the bed "I know you don't want to marry him my love, but now more than ever we need a good alliance to help us beat the lycans." He said, his voice gentle which just irritated Faylan even more "So my love and happiness are irrelevant to you?"

"No, of course not but we just can't afford to think like that right now." His voice pained as if it physically hurt him to say those words. She sighed, he really did care for her feelings but had a duty to perform as king to protect his people and couldn't afford any weaknesses. She sat up as she said, "That woman in court yesterday was very charming." She was anxious about his reaction and he chuckled "Very high standing amongst the witches too, unfortunately, you will never be allowed to marry a woman, your mother would never allow it, you would have to leave here in order to do that." He explained, almost knowing what she was implying about herself "I want you to be happy my love but not at the expense of your safety, if you wish to engage in this type of thing, keep it secret, for both of your sakes." He said gently as he got up, smiling softly at her. This gave her some hope, that at least one of her parents accepted it if she wanted to love another woman, it was her mother that she had to be careful of, she was all about tradition and honouring the family name, and marrying a woman would be a dishonour to the family. Her mother already didn't love her or like her as much as she did her twin, Faylan was pretty sure that if he wanted to love another man, her mother would have accepted it but because she was inferior because she was a woman. She sighed as she got up, getting ready for the day, excited at the thought of seeing Eliana again but worried about what was happening with the marriage to Nikolas and the war that was inevitably coming but most importantly, seeing her mother, knowing now that she was not supportive of same-sex couples or anyone who is not completely straight. She sighed as her father left the room, allowing her to get ready for the day, she chose a pair of black pants, a white shirt, and her black boots, walking downstairs, ignoring her mother's looks of incredulity. She always had to wear dresses unless she was on a horse but today, she felt defiant, excited, and eager to start her training with Eliana but she had to have family breakfast first, gods she hated it, her mother watched her from across the table as she ate, her father looked over at Faylan and a smirk formed on his lips, knowing she was doing this to annoy her mother. Faylan focused on her food, not looking up till she was finished, she looked at her father "May I be excused?" She asked and he nodded, watching her leave before bearing the wrath of her mother's shouts of anger at what she was wearing. Faylan chuckled to herself as she walked outside to the stables, checking on her horse Thunder, as she always did whenever she had the time. She greeted the stable hands and gently stroked Thunder's mane, feeding him an apple with her other hand. Making sure no one was listening, she started to talk to him about her conundrum, her sexuality, Eliana and her mother, and the wedding, sighing as she finished "Feels like you're the only one that listens to me" she smiled as Thunder bumped his head gently into her, almost trying to comfort her and tell her that he cared for her and her feelings.

She left the stables after about half an hour and wandered through the gardens, hoping to bump into Eliana as she'd realised, they'd never said where to meet but she would find her, she needed to, it was as though her heart yearned for her, to be in her presence and not just for a short time but for as long as possible. "Looking for someone?" Nikolas' voice came from the bench behind her, she turned around and chuckled "No, just going for a walk, what are you doing out here?" She asked as she sat next to him and he snorted "I needed to get away from my parents and their incessant talk of marriage and heirs, it was giving me a headache." He rubbed his temple and looked at her "The woman yesterday, Eliana, wasn't it? She seemed to have an effect on you" he chuckled mischievously and she playfully rolled her eyes "I don't quite know what you mean"

"You can tell me, it's just us out here" he smiled and she chuckled "Fine, yes, she did attract me but it's not like anything can come from it, my mother is too traditional and doesn't like people who aren't straight, she'd disown me." She sighed and Nikolas gently took her hand "Faylan, yes family is important but so are you and your happiness, what's eternity if you're not happy? you need to find what makes you happy and keep hold of it, no matter how much people try and take it from you, it's your life milady, you choose your own fate." He smiled at her and she knew he was right but she was so terrified to follow her heart and train, be a soldier and a practitioner of magic, and pursue Eliana and see where it goes. She smiled at him "You're right, maybe you should take your own advice and go be happy with that girl at home, come back to visit me of course, I wish to meet her one day." She giggled and he blushed "I will try." He smiled at her and glanced behind her "Well, I think it's time I take my leave." He smiled and got up, bowing slightly "See you later princess." he said as he walked off, Faylan watched him go, looking out at the gardens, unaware that Eliana was behind her, watching her. She went over and sat next to her "Enjoying the view?" she joked and Faylan gasped "You scared me"

"You should have heard me coming, with your elf ears and all." She chuckled, she was right of course, Elves were known for their excellent hearing and being able to hear over long distances. Faylan giggled "Maybe I chose not to hear you." She said and looked at her, she was wearing a red shirt and black leather pants that showed off her figure, she obviously wasn't ashamed of the way she looked, unlike Faylan who had a hard time looking at herself in the mirror most days. Eliana smiled and shook her head "I know how your parents feel about you learning to fight and learning about war in general but, if you don't mind me saying, any future queen should be ready for anything, and with these Lycans…anything can happen, for the first time in my life, I'm unsure what the future holds and whether we'll live to see next spring." She sighed, the stress of the situation was evident from her tired eyes and slightly shaking fingers. Faylan felt sad for her, she knew that the coming war would not just affect the elves but everyone, and that must be causing a lot of stress for her as she had to think about not just her people but everyone. Faylan looked at Eliana "I am sure everything will turn out okay, our species has survived centuries of war, and I am sure we can survive one more." She tried to sound optimistic and Eliana smiled "Thank you for trying to make me feel better, I am sure you're right." She tried to feel optimistic but Faylan could tell that she wasn't sure if everything was going to be okay, for all they knew, their whole lives could be over in a few months, their homes could be destroyed or, worst case scenario, they could die, their families could die and this thought terrified Faylan and she could tell that Eliana was terrified to so she decided to change the subject "so, what are you going to teach me today?" she chuckled and Eliana perked up at that and smiled "I was thinking we start of easy, like moving things with your magic or changing the colour of something." She suggested and I nodded eagerly and she chuckled "Alright, let's get started."

They practiced for a few hours with a lot of failures and frustration but Eliana was always patient and kind whenever she didn't achieve. Faylan eventually managed to lift the apple off the ground and she squealed with happiness, Eliana clapped and smiled at her, her red eyes sparkling in the setting sunlight. She looked beautiful in the orange light, Faylan's breath hitched every time she looked at her, she had to admit she was starting to fall for this woman and it had only been a day. She lowered the apple back onto the floor and Eliana smiled "Well done! That was really good for the first day." She chuckled as Faylan blushed lightly at the praise "Thank you, I was worried I wouldn't be able to do it."

"It was amazing that you could do that within a few hours of teaching, most people struggle a lot with it, this shows me that you have a talent for magic." Eliana smiled and Faylan nodded "Must be because I'm an elf."

"That does help, yes." Eliana admitted, "But that is not the only reason you are able to pick magic up so quickly, it could be in your genes or maybe you're just smarter than other people." She chuckled and Faylan giggled "I'll take the fact that I'm smarter, sounds better." She giggled and Eliana smiled, looking at her, she couldn't tell what she was thinking as she looked at her, it was the only time she couldn't read her so she decided to ask "What are you thinking about?"

"You." She said, very matter of fact, and smiled "You intrigue me, you're not like any elf I've ever met before, you are kind, your heart is pure, and not many people have that nowadays and it draws me in."

"Really?" she questioned, "my mother is not the most welcoming individual since my brother died, she hates me so, everyone else has no chance." She chuckled but her tone was a little sad at the thought and Eliana gently took her hand "I am so sorry; I wish I could help you; no mother should treat their child that way so they believe that they are hated. It is not fair; you deserve to be loved and valued and treated the way you should be." She said, her voice genuine and kind as she spoke, making Faylan feel almost weak in the knees. She snapped back to reality and looked at her "thank you, I hope one day I get to experience that." She smiled and Eliana smiled back "I am sure you will, just know that I am always here for you if you ever need to talk about anything or even just to take your mind off things." Faylan smiled at her as a thank you just as Nikolas ran over to them, a worried look on his face as he tried to catch his breath, Eliana looked up at him as she let go of Faylan's hand "Nikolas? What's going on?" She asked, now getting a little worried herself. Once he'd caught his breath, Nikolas said, "The lycans, they've attacked Moroza, there were no survivors." His voice sounded sad when he said this, Moroza was a small village where a coven of Lunar witches was. The last village that contained their kind...the Lunar witches were officially, and devastatingly, extinct.

Chapter 4

The news of the massacre spread fast through the witch community. Eliana went back to her people to grieve, much to Faylan's sadness but she understood, that her people came first. No matter how hard she tried, Faylan couldn't seem to find enjoyment in any of her activities now that Eliana was gone. Nikolas tried to cheer her up, the two had become good friends in the few weeks since Eliana had left. Their parents had postponed their 'wedding' out of respect for the witches and their losses.

"I can't take this tension anymore" Faylan groaned as she sat next to Nikolas on the grass "I hate that they're still trying to go ahead with the wedding after everything that's happened and is going to happen." She looked at him and he shrugged "They want to put their stupid traditions first, they'll see, and it'll blow back in their faces." He said as he laid down on his back, Faylan joining him as they looked up at the clouds passing overhead. Faylan didn't want it to happen but she knew it would, she knew that her parents not focusing on the real issue at hand was going to blow up in their faces, she just didn't know how yet but she wanted to try to get ahead of it and figure it out so she could stop it happening. Nikolas looked at her, almost knowing what she was thinking "I'll help you do whatever needs to be done, no matter the cost, for my people and more importantly, yours." He smiled at her and she smiled back, looking back up at the sky before her view was blocked by her mother "Nice to see the two of you getting along." She said, her voice almost patronising as she spoke to them, making Faylan want to roll her eyes but she put on a smile and said "Yes mother, now what is it you want?" she asked, Nikolas had to hide his snort of laughter when he heard the same patronising tone from Faylan as she spoke. Her mother ignored it and looked at Nikolas "The king wants to talk to you in the throne room and I would like to talk to my daughter, alone." She said, looking down at them and Nikolas got up and gave a short bow "Of course Your Majesty." He said, giving Faylan a small smile as he walked back to the castle. She sat up as her mother sat down on a bench opposite her "What is it mother? What have I done now?" she said as she brushed the leaves out of her hair. Her mother sighed and looked at her "Why have you been spending time with that witch? And communicating with her?"

"Because she is my friend, mother, is that such a crime?" Faylan replied in frustration and her mother frowned at her "Those witches are volatile, unpredictable, and dangerous. I am trying to look out for you." This made Faylan laugh the most sarcastic laugh she could, taking her mother by surprise "Looking out for me? You don't care for me or what I want and need, you only care about tradition and what you want, you have since my brother died, you don't love me like you did him and I've accepted that but what I won't stand for is you trying to force a life on me that I don't want." She said, taking a deep breath when she finished, feeling a weight lift from her shoulders as she finally told her mother how she made her feel. Her mother just looked at her, a look of shock on her face, trying to figure out what to say or to retaliate, her face showed this internal war on what to do. Faylan stood up, brushing her pants off "Exactly." She said as she walked off toward the Flower Maze at the end of the gardens. Her mother eventually got up and caught up to her, grabbing her arm to stop them from walking "I am sorry Faylan but you know how important our traditions are to your father and me" Faylan shook her head "Father doesn't care, he wants me to be happy which is what you should want, as my mother, that is all you should care about." She spat and got out of her grip, storming off back to the castle, locking herself in her room in a rage.

A few hours later she heard a knock at the door and her father's voice saying "Fay? Can you unlock the door for me?" he asked, his voice gentle as she got up from her reading chair by the window and walked to the door, sighing as she slid the lock open and walked back to the chair, placing the blanket back over her legs "what is it father?" she asked, trying to keep the sound of annoyance out of her voice as she wasn't annoyed at him and it wouldn't be fair. Her father came into her room and sat on the windowsill, looking at her "My love…I know you're unhappy about this whole arrangement and now your mother knows exactly how you feel, about everything and she's not happy, she wants you to comply and do what's being asked of you but just because of this, it doesn't mean she doesn't love you."

"Yes, it does, she never loved me as much as she did Taeral, she always wanted sons, not a daughter. I'm just a huge disappointment to her." She sighed and looked out the window, the clouds had turned grey, a storm was coming and a big one, she could feel it. Elves were very in tune with nature and could feel when something was about to happen. Her father's look was one of kindness and a small degree of pain, Faylan imagined it was because she had brought up her brother. It was a painful topic for all of her family but no one felt it like she did, she felt the life drain from his body, she felt his fear. No one understood the pain she went through every day and the nightmares his loss had caused her. Her father sighed "I know that's how it seems but I promise it's not true." He said, ignoring her scoff as he continued "You are our daughter Faylan, we love you just as much as we do your brother and we would subject him to this tradition as well as it's the way it's been since our creation."

"Yes, but that doesn't mean they're outdated and should be changed." She said, exasperated and he nodded "I know, I agree but your mother doesn't, so we have to do it, I am sorry." He got up and went to kiss her head but she moved her head away, he stepped back, hurt as he left the room, leaving Faylan alone with her thoughts and anger, making her want to run, run away from her family and their outdated traditions, away from the impending war, to wherever Eliana was now. She missed her. The way she laughed, the way she scrunched her nose when she smiled, the way she understood. She looked out at the setting sun, a plan starting to hatch in her mind. She made her way to Nikolas's room, knocking on the door. He opened it and looked at it "Faylan? What is it? What's wrong?" he asked, the friendly concern in his voice very visible as he looked at her. She looked up at him "We leave at midnight, make sure you pack everything you need; we're going on an adventure." A mischievous grin spread across his face as she looked at him, a cheeky smile on her face and an adventurous twinkle in her eye.

Chapter 5

The world outside the elf kingdom was new to Faylan. It fascinated her as she was so used to the beauty and elegance of her kingdom. Nikolas met her in the clearing in the woods where she had told him to meet her and smiled "Where we going then princess?" he teased her with the nickname and she rolled her eyes, chuckling as she started walking "anywhere but here." She was dressed in comfortable pants, a shirt, and boots. Nikolas looked at her, thinking how those clothes suited her much more than the big, puffy dresses that her mother made her wear. Faylan led the way out of the forest that she knew like the back of her hand but after that, it was all new territory to her. Nikolas took over from there "I can't take you to my kingdom, my parents and yours will be looking for us soon, I'll take you to some witches I know, they'll help us, keep us safe." He said and Faylan nodded, hoping he meant Eliana but she knew it was a long shot, she'd never told them where she was from so they had no way of finding her, unless she found them.

She lost track of how long they were walking for, as she was looking at her surroundings. She bumped into Nikolas, who had stopped walking, and looked up at him "Why have we stopped?" she asked, secretly thanking every Creator that they had finally stopped walking, her feet aching in her leather boots. Nikolas gently grabbed her chin and turned it towards a gushing waterfall. It was stunning. It took her breath away as she looked at it, she had seen waterfalls before but nothing like this, it had something mystical about it with the rainbow showing in the spray, and the strange flowers growing in the brush at the base of it. There were all manners of creatures milling around the falls, some grazing in the grass, bathing in the sun, or drinking from the pool at the bottom of the waterfall. Nikolas looked down at her, smiling at her awe of the sight before them. He was used to this but he knew that Faylan wasn't and he had to admit, her fascination and giddy excitement was adorable. He started to walk forward, breaking her out of her trance, jogging to catch up to him. He headed straight for the falls and Faylan looked at him, confused "What are you doing?"

"Just trust me." He smiled at her and kept going, the spray from the falls starting to hit them as they got closer, the cool water a sweet release from the heat around them. They kept walking through the falls, getting soaked before they made it to a cave behind the falls and Faylan chuckled "If this is where you murder me, it's very unimaginative." She said nervously and Nikolas just smiled and kept walking through the cave, Faylan at his side. After about 5 minutes, they made it to the other side of the cave, it was an opening seemingly covered by some form of foliage, Nikolas pushed it aside for her and she exited the cave, the sight that met her was one of pure beauty and wonder. In front of her was a huge clearing, a huge castle in the middle of it, and small cottages dotted around the rest of the clearing. The castle seemed to be made of some form of silk but Faylan knew that was impossible and that it was just a trick of the light and was probably made from marble or stone. There were all kinds of creatures roaming around the clearing, Faylan saw a hawk that looked to be the same size as the highest peak of the castle and a deer with 2 heads, a wolf with the head of a snake. These creatures unnerved her but fascinated her, she wondered how they came to be, she theorised experimentation or magic or simply genetics and forced breeding. As they started to walk down the paved path to the castle, they were followed by a huge dog, it looked like a mixture of a wolf and an Alsatian, it was pretty cute she had to admit. Nikolas smiled at the creature, fished a steak out of his backpack, and tossed it to it, the creature's tail wagging happily as it ate "Seems we made a friend." He chuckled and nudged Faylan who was watching the creature, gently petting its head and smiling. She noticed Nikolas had walked off and she caught up to him "This place is amazing." She said and he chuckled "It is, isn't it? The witches who live here are the Lunar witches, this area is a hotspot for their magic and they're hidden from the rest of the world so they can live in peace." He explained as they made their way to the doors of the castle. They opened as a witch came out, like they were automatic "What are you doing here Nikolas?"

"We need a safe place to stay for a while." Nikolas said, Faylan standing beside him, her long hair covering her elf ears "We're looking for someone." He said, looking at Faylan "She's a friend of ours and we haven't heard from her for a while and we want to know that she is okay." He finished and the witch looked at them, looking Faylan up and down, almost trying to figure out what she was. Faylan looked down at her boots and sighed, tucking her hair behind her ears out of habit and the witch smiled "You're an elf?"

"Yes, my name is Faylan Rohana." She said and the other girl chuckled "You're looking for Eliana Creighton."

"You know her?" Nikolas cut in and she nodded "Yes, she passed through here a few days ago, she stayed for a night before moving on." She said and motioned to the doors "Come inside, we can talk more in there, this conversation is best had away from eavesdropping ears." She said and led them into the main area of the castle, Faylan looked around her as she walked. It was just as beautiful on the inside as it was on the outside, there was gold circling the ceiling and there were statues dotted all over the place, seemingly without any real reason for their placement. She followed the others into the main area, there was a huge, round table in the centre of the room with food and places set with plates for 3 people. She didn't even question why it was already set for 3 people, they were in witch territory after all, all she was thinking about was how hungry she was, she hadn't realised it until she smelled the chicken and ham that were out on the table. Her stomach growled loudly, making the witch chuckle "Someone's hungry." She said as she sat down "apologies, I didn't introduce myself, my name is Serene." She smiled at them as they sat down and Faylan smiled at her, helping herself to some food before looking at her "How do you know Eliana?"

"All witches know the Dark Arts witches, they are the most powerful of us and the most dangerous, after our Civil War a few centuries ago, most Witches still don't trust them, Lunar Witches are one of the very few kinds of Witches that do trust and work with them. Eliana is a good friend of mine and I just want to be there for her after she lost her birthplace and if I can help her friends to find her and make sure she's okay, then I will." She said, "I am worried for her as she seemed very broken and like she wants vengeance for what happened and that is a dangerous combination for a Dark Arts witch."

She poured herself a drink and looked at Faylan and Nikolas. Nikolas sighed, knitting his hands together in front of him "I think that Faylan and I want to find her for slightly different reasons but for me, it is to make sure she is okay and see if she will help me and my love make a new life away from my family's oppression." He said, fiddling with the bracelet on his wrist and Selene smiled at him "she and I are the best people to ask for this type of dilemma." She looked at Faylan "what about you?"

"I want to just get her back." She said, looking at her plate "I really care about her and I just want her back." Selene smiled at her as if she knew what she meant. Even though she was away from her family, she still didn't want to admit that she liked her, she could hear her brother in her head saying 'Stop being a scaredy cat and face this, say it, what's the worst that could happen?' she smiled a little to herself at the thought and hid it in her drink. She looked at Selene "So can you help us?"

"Of course, I can, you are more than welcome to stay in the castle, we have a lot of spare rooms and training grounds if you need them." She said and clasped her hands together "Eliana mentioned how she was teaching Faylan magic and if you are still interested then I can help further your knowledge." She offered, looking at Faylan. Faylan looked at her hands, nodding "I'd like that" She smiled at her and Nikolas cleared his throat "Well I'm going to get some rest, I'm exhausted, I'll leave you to it." He smiled at them and gave Faylan a short bow before leaving the room, going to find a bedroom for himself. Selene let Faylan finish her food before she stood up and said "Shall we go get started?" she smiled as she got up with a small grin on her face "Lead the way." She followed her outside, butterflies in her stomach, feeling closer to Eliana again as the lesson started.

Chapter 6

Over the next few months, Selene taught Faylan how to use her elf magic properly and to its highest potential. Nikolas on the other hand, was working on his physical combat, teaching the basics to Faylan when she asked. Faylan was getting stronger, putting on a bit of muscle, and becoming more athletic. Elves are naturally very light-footed and fast but Faylan wasn't very athletic and strong until now as she was used simply as a pretty face back in her homeland. She loved the fact that she could now protect herself, that she didn't need her parents or some man to protect her from the bad things. She could do that herself. She sighed happily as she lay back in the bath, enjoying the warmth and relief that came with nursing her aches, pains, and bruises from a long day of training. The foam added a bit more privacy and the calming lavender smell from the salts helped to ease her overworked mind. She closed her eyes as she lay in the warm water, her mind drifting to Eliana, how much she missed her and was dying to see her again. Faylan missed the feeling of safety and acceptance she gave her and how kind and stunningly beautiful she was. Her mind also drifted to her parents, as it often did. She thought about what had happened since she left. Had they looked for her? Had they forgotten her? No, her father wouldn't do that. Surely, they would have sent out search parties by now, unless they thought she was dead. As horrible as it sounded to her, she was glad that they thought that, it gave her a chance to be free, to be who she wanted to be without her mother forcing her to be what she wasn't.

Eventually, she got out when the water started to get cold. Shivering a little, she dried herself and got dressed into her black leather pants and a red button shirt. A knock came at the door, Nikolas's voice coming through the door "Can I enter?" he asked, polite as ever and she nodded "Yes" She sat on the bed, her notebook out before her with all her combat and magic notes in. Nikolas walked in and moved one of the chairs close to the bed, sitting on it, they were close but he didn't believe they were 'sitting on each other's beds' close. He looked at her, an unreadable expression on his face which made her instantly worried, she hated not being able to read his expression "What's wrong Nik?" she asked, closing her notebooks, her full attention on him. He sighed and looked at his hands, playing with one of his many rings "There has been word that the Lycans have invaded and wiped out a vampire nest in the west, I am not sure which one but I will need to leave for a while to check on my people."

"of course, I'll be safe here and I'll keep looking for Eliana and if I find anything, I'll send a message." She said, a sad smile on her face, he looked up at her, his dark eyes unsure. He took a deep breath "Anything happens, anything at all, you run and don't stop, okay?" his tone suddenly serious and he sounded just like one of the soldiers from her home, she gently took his hand in hers "I promise." He looked at their hands and smiled a little "Good, I know it's going to be hard but try to stay out of trouble." He playfully dug and she scoffed and playfully pushed his hand away "I am offended by the fact you think I purposely get myself into trouble, I just seem to attract it." She giggled and he smiled "I am afraid that appears to be true." He chuckled and looked at her, his look unreadable, it seemed to be a mixture between sadness and anger but there also seemed to be a hint of affection in his eyes. She didn't know whether this was towards her or not but she didn't ask, they were best friends and always would be. He stood up, giving a short bow before she looked up at him "You don't need to do that, I'm not a princess here, just an elf who is unqualified for this war and wants a chance at survival and love." She smiled up at him and he nodded "I like this new side to you, the warrior, the woman your mother was afraid you would become. This version of you…" he paused and looked at her "Has the biggest chance of surviving this war, becoming the best queen and woman you could possibly be." He smiled at her before walking out of the room, leaving her to think about what he just said. He was, of course, right. She was a lot more likely to survive now that she knew how to, she always hated the long ball gowns and the galas to show her off to potential suitors but she didn't mind it when the dances were just for the fun of having a dance, those were usually arranged by her father and didn't have as many, if any, rules. These types of events tended to happen when her mother was away as she and her father both knew she would severely disapprove and never allow it to happen.

Nikolas left the next morning, and Faylan had got up early to say goodbye to him. It was going to be strange without him around to teach her things or even just to sit with, in the sun while she read a book and he tried to sunbathe but of course, being a vampire, he was always going to be very pale as he was technically dead. She watched him ride away, a wave of sadness coming over her as Selene put a hand on her shoulder "he'll be back don't worry, he's a strong one." She smiled gently at her and

Faylan nodded, trying to believe her, Nikolas was a strong man, he was centuries old and probably the best fighter she'd met in her lifetime. She walked back inside, picking up an apple and a sandwich before grabbing her notebook and sitting outside on the grass, drawing in the sunshine, trying to ignore the crushing loneliness that was weighing her down. She knew he would be back soon and had only left an hour ago but she suddenly realised just how alone she was in the world without Nikolas, Eliana, or her parents. She sighed softly, drawing in her notebook as she thought about the reason she ran away. She wanted to escape a forced marriage yes, but was all of this worth it? All the death and worry she'd probably caused her parents when they woke up to her being gone. She also wanted to find Eliana but what if she didn't want it to be found? What if she didn't like her back?

What if she did? How would they move forward in such an uncertain world? The threat of war is constantly around them and their obligation to their people still swirling around their heads. So many questions were circling Faylan's head and none had any answers and this frustrated her. She hated not knowing but there was also a certain thrill that came with the unknown, her whole life had been dictated for her but now she had no idea what would happen next, or even if she would survive this war. She pushed that thought from her mind and focussed on drawing the tree in front of her.

After a few hours of drawing and sitting in the sun, she started to hear some commotion coming from one of the small villages. She got up and looked around, walking towards the noise which she quickly realised was screaming. She started to run. The site that met her eyes was like a nightmare. Fires were spreading through the houses, the thatched roofs completely alight, panicked families running from their homes screaming and crying. Children were cowering behind things, confused and afraid. She then noticed who set the fires, there was a group of men and women, dressed in some form of armour, nothing she'd seen before. Their eyes seemed to glow from behind their hoods, all she could see were their bright yellow eyes. She didn't notice the creature sneaking up behind her until it was too late and it pounced.

Chapter 7

The creature pinned her down, its jaws locking tightly around her leg. She screamed in pain and used her free leg to kick at the creature. It eventually let go and she flipped over onto her back, her vision foggy from the loss of blood from the gaping wound in her leg. It was then she realised what the creature was. A lycan. It was big, much bigger than any others she'd seen before. It was jet black and had bright yellow eyes, her blood dripping from its mouth as it turned back round to face her, a row of sharp jagged teeth became visible as it snarled at her. A loud voice snapped something at it and it backed away, its head bowed, almost like how one might bow to royalty. A tall blonde man walked toward Faylan, the lycans moving out of the way 'he must be some sort of royalty to them' she thought 'a prince maybe? Or a king?' she wasn't sure if they had royalty but clearly, they had some form of hierarchy. She looked up at the man, noticing his features a lot more now he was closer, he had strikingly blue eyes, a well-structured face, and cheekbones that looked like they could cut someone just by touching them but the most eye-catching thing of all were the 3 huge scars across his face, surprisingly they'd missed his eye. He squatted down in front of her, grabbing her wounded leg, making her hiss loudly in pain. He seemed to enjoy seeing her in pain as a small smirk appeared on his face as he moved her hair back behind her ears, showing their points. He grinned at her when he saw them, not a nice grin though, an evil, snarky grin "I see we have ourselves an elf." He sneered, his grip on her leg tightened, making her growl lowly. He removed his hand from her leg, it was covered in her blood. He brought a finger to his lips, a long black tongue coming out, licking the blood from it. A strange expression crossed his face, one she couldn't quite decipher as he stood up, wiping his hand on his trouser leg, talking indistinctly to one of the men standing behind him and he walked off, the blonde man walking back over to her "my name is Darion, I am the general of this pack and the crowned prince of all Lycans, I imagine you've heard of me." His narcissism was on full display and it took everything in her power not to roll her eyes at him, she just said "Unfortunately, I have not had the unpleasure" She looked up at him, trying to hide the disdain in her voice. His head whipped around as she said this, surprise and hatred in his eyes "Of course not, you elves are so sheltered and ignorant to the world outside your fancy castles and palaces." He spat, forcing her to bite the inside of her mouth to stop her from retorting back with something that would definitely earn her a beating. He was of course right, not that she'd ever tell him that. She just looked up at him with a death glare, trying not to show her fear but she knew that if he focused enough, he could smell it, she hoped he wasn't doing that now. She looked up at him, dragging herself up onto her elbows, her vision becoming blurrier as she lost more and more blood by the second. Darion said something to the man next to him before walking off. The man started to walk closer to Faylan, a sword in his hand, he raised it, and she closed her eyes as he waited for him to strike when he gasped and gurgled in apparent pain. She opened her eyes and looked up and saw the man's heart fly out of his chest, his body slumping to the ground, revealing Selene, the blue glow of her magic fading as she ran to her, wrapping her leg in a tight bandage, keeping the other lycans off them with a barrier of magic around them. Now she was closer Faylan could see that she was covered in blood and had a deep gash in her forehead that was still bleeding a little bit. She noticed she had armour on and a sword strapped to her hip. She looked at Faylan "It's going to hurt but you're going to need to run."

"What about you?" She asked, her voice shaking a little as she looked up at her. Selene helped her up "I'll be fine, you need to run, it's you they're after, they want an elf as leverage against your kind." She explained, "To force your armies to stand down." Faylan mulled this over, did this mean that elves were attacking Lycan strongholds? Maybe, why else would they be so desperate for leverage? She thought about how Darion looked when he tasted her blood, maybe he could taste the royalty in her blood if that was even possible. She snapped back to reality when she realised Selene was attaching her armour to her and strapping her sword to her hip "You need these" she protested, trying to stop her. She just swatted her hands away "You will need them more than me, I am just a pawn on this chessboard, you are the queen." She said before looking her in the eyes "Stay alive." She pushed her backward gently "Now run" she dropped the barrier "Run!" she shouted at her and she stumbled backward, running as fast as she could, which was more of a fast limp, away. She looked back, seeing sparks of blue flying out from where Selene was. She felt a hand grab her arm as she stopped running, dragging her forward "Come on! You can't stop running!" a familiar voice said firmly, it took her a moment to clear her thoughts and realise who it was "Eliana" she breathed out, the taller girl smiled down at her "hello Faylan, we can catch up later, right now we need to run" she said, using her magic to keep any lycans at bay, red streaks of magic flying out of her fingers "what about Selene?" Faylan asked, looking back to see her getting surrounded. Eliana's eyes went sad as she said "There's nothing we can do, we can run, find Nikolas."

"We have to try and do something" she cried out but as the words left her lips, a scream came from Selene, her head looked in her direction and she saw blood flying everywhere. She froze, processing what she had just seen and heard. She was dead. Selene was dead. She barely noticed Eliana dragging her away into the woods surrounding the settlement, she felt numb but she could feel her hands shaking, she didn't know if it was from shock or rage, the two emotions seemed to blur into one. She must have blacked out because when she came to, she was sat down by a small fire, a big coat wrapped around her, only then did she notice how cold it was. Eliana came back over to her, a small rabbit in her hand "Ah, you're awake" she said gently, her tone a little light-hearted. This annoyed Faylan a little, how could she be joking when who knows how many people just died? Including Selene, someone she considered a friend. As though she read her mind, Eliana said "If I don't joke around, I'll cry and I've done enough of that lately." She looked down, Faylan noticing that she had definitely lost weight and there were red rings around her eyes from where she'd been crying. Faylan looked down, feeling sad that she hadn't been able to be there for her to help her through her grief. She moved closer to her, gently wrapping her arms around her, hoping to give her some sort of comfort. Eliana carefully hugged back, sighing softly as she buried her face in her neck, a wave of safety washing over her. She felt all the bad emotions and events of the last few months came flooding back, though she refused to cry. She was fed up with crying, of feeling helpless, she wanted to do something about this mess, the war, how Faylan must feel, and how alone she must feel. She was a Dark Arts witch for goodness sake. She sighed, moving back from Faylan, her mind racing. She looked at Faylan, her trousers covered in mud and dried blood, her face pale, and her hair messy and tangled. Without saying anything, she picked up a bundle of spare clothes she had with her "Take these and go and change, I'll change your bandage after." She said gently and Faylan nodded, shaking as she got up and went behind a tree to get changed, limping back out 5 minutes later. She sat back down next to the fire, trying to warm up as she realised how cold she was as the adrenaline wore off. Eliana moved close to her and lifted her trouser leg up so she could change the bandage on her wound. Once she had changed it, she rolled her trouser leg back down and gently set her leg back down "There, good as new." She partly joked, not really wanting to expose just how bad her leg looked. Faylan let out a quiet chuckle and went back to looking at the fire, seemingly getting lost in her thoughts. She didn't ask her what she was thinking about, she didn't want to upset her so she just cooked one of the animals she'd hunted earlier. Faylan fiddled with her sleeves, bringing them down so they covered her hands "I want to find Nik" she said after a few moments of silence, making Eliana turn to look at her and nod a little "I know and we will, did he say anything about where he was going?" she asked and Faylan shook her head "no, just that one of the vampire nests out west had been attacked." She said quietly, not looking at her, watching the fire crackle and flicker. Eliana rummaged through her bag and found a map, it had all the witch villages and strongholds on it and Faylan's home and known elf cities, not a lot of people knew where they all were they prided themselves on secrecy, especially after the first war with the lycans, it also showed all the vampire nests on it, that they knew about. Eliana started to mark out all the places where a vampire nest could be on the west side of the map. She marked out 3 places in total, chewing the top of her oak wood pencil when she'd finished "We'll head up to the first area I've marked tomorrow. For now, have something to eat and rest, I'll keep watch." She said gently, folding the map up and putting it and the pencil back in her bag. Faylan looked at the food and sighed, after everything she'd seen and been through in the last few hours, she had no appetite. She decided to just lay down and try to get some sleep. Eventually, she drifted into an uncomfortable sleep filled with nightmares, blood, and bodies.

~~~~~

She woke to a hand covering her mouth. Her eyes went wide. Once she realised it was just Eliana with a finger to her lips, she calmed down "lycans" she whispered, "We need to go, now." She removed her hand from her mouth and grabbed her bag as Faylan got up and grabbed her weapons and jacket. As soon as they started to walk, Eliana realised that she wasn't limping anymore and so she questioned it "You're not limping anymore, is your leg better?" Faylan looked at her "It doesn't hurt anymore if that's what you

mean" she replied, a little
confused, glancing down at her leg.
She brushed the confusion off and
kept walking, putting the sudden
lack of pain down to the fact she
was immortal. It didn't make sense
though. She'd seen her father with
injuries that lasted weeks, not less
than 24 hours. Her mind was
racing and she was so confused,
nothing made sense. The only
thing that did make sense was her
feelings for Eliana and how much
she cared for Nikolas. She looked
at Eliana as they walked, her red
eyes were glinting in the morning
sun, the sunlight bouncing off her
jewellery and making her dark hair
sparkle in the light. She looked
beautiful. More than beautiful. She
dared not tell her, now was not the
time to confess her feelings, there
were bigger issues to deal with,
like finding Nikolas and ending the
war between her people and the
lycans.

They walked for a few days before they came upon the first of the 3 nests they were going to search for Nikolas. They cautiously make their way into the pitch-black cave. It was oddly quiet. Faylan had thought there would at least be someone on watch, especially with what was going on in the world. Eliana lit a torch she found on the floor and they were greeted with a terrible sight. Everyone was dead. Their heads had been removed and left on spikes, almost like a warning to anyone coming in. The smell was overwhelming, causing Eliana to cover her nose and mouth, gagging a little at it. Faylan was in a state of shock as she noticed that a lot of the people in this nest had been children. She ran out of the cave, gagging and vomiting on the ground outside, coughing and retching. Eliana came out a few minutes later, a few journals in her hands "Are you alright?" she asked, concerned and

Faylan nodded "Yeah, it was just the smell." She sighed, sitting down on a rock and looking at the journals "What did you find?"

"I'm not sure yet," Eliana said, glancing down at them "but we should get somewhere safer before we look through them, just in case anyone comes back, those spikes were a warning." She said, confirming Faylan's theory. Faylan nodded and got up, wiping her mouth, the taste of bile was strong in her mouth and the smell of the corpses forever burned into her nose as she walked with Eliana to find somewhere safe to set up camp for the night.

Once they'd lit a fire and had some food, they started to look through the journals. Eliana took one and Faylan took the other. As Faylan looked through hers, she found an entry from the day before the massacre

"They have been watching us for weeks, trying to figure out how many of us there are. They're waiting to attack; I can sense it. We need to get the women and children to safety, anywhere but here will do, maybe I'll send them to the witches. They will look after them, they have looked after our Prince Nikolas for the last few months. He came to see us, to make sure we were okay. He mentioned about an elf princess who ran away in search of a crush. Elves and their ridiculous fantasies. I can smell the Lycans. They're closer. If you're reading this, we're probably all dead, I hope we can get them out

-D"

Faylan read it again and sighed, wondering what they meant by 'elves and their ridiculous fantasies'. Are the elves not allowed to be happy? Or is it just that a lot of elves are passive and won't fight in this war as they don't want to get hurt? That's probably what they meant. She didn't want to be like those elves, she wanted to make her parents proud, she wanted to be a warrior but she also wanted to be happy and maybe marry and have children one day. She needed to survive this war first. She needed to be the warrior her mother never wanted her to be. She needed to develop a stomach for violence to protect those she loved but also herself. She needed to be ruthless.

Chapter 8

They searched the second nest marked on the map the following day. Faylan had a little bit more hope as this nest was still alive, even if it was on high alert due to the attack on the first nest. Faylan looked around as they were led through to the leader, it was filled with vampires, almost to the point where she felt claustrophobic because of how crowded it was. She saw soldiers everywhere, sorting through weapons and armour. They gave her a dirty look as she walked past, almost as though she was the cause of all their suffering. She instinctively covered her pointed ears with her hair, though she couldn't change her height and the fact she made barely any noise as she walked.

They were led into what looked like a war room, she could tell by the big table in the middle with little figurines positioned on the map to show where all the nests were and where the enemy was. She glanced around the room, jumping a little at the guard who was standing right next to the door, she hadn't even noticed him when she walked in. She stood close to Eliana as they walked into the centre of the room, their weapons removed from them as the leader stood up, looking at them. The leader made a hand motion and everyone left the room, leaving the girls at her mercy. She looked them up and down and leaned against the table "Well then? What is it that you want?" she asked, raising an eyebrow. Eliana moved forward a step "Ma'am, we are looking for a vampire named Nikolas, do you know where he is?" she asked politely. The leader chuckled a little "Ah Nikolas, he was here a few days ago, he never said where he was going" She looked at Faylan "It was brave of you to bring an elf into my home, considering it is their fault we're being brought into this mess." She said, her voice filled with venom as she spoke causing Faylan to look at the floor, a feeling of shame washing over her. Eliana noticed and took her hand as reassurance "In her defence, she's on our side, she wants nothing to do with this war." She said defensively and the woman chuckled "You better be telling the truth, if not, she will go down with her people and the lycans." She walked around the table and sat down "My name is Marla, I can give you supplies and send you in the direction Nikolas probably will have gone but you cannot stay here much longer, my people do not like the elves as it is and they will question my leadership if I am seen to be siding with one."

"So, power means more to you than the lives of the helpless?" Eliana said. Helpless, a word

Faylan didn't want to be associated with but she stayed quiet, thinking it best not to argue with someone who already disliked her just for what she was. Marla looked at her "That's not true, we are just not in a position to hold an election right now as it will ruin our chances of survival if we are already fighting amongst ourselves." She sighed and looked at Faylan "I want peace between us all but I know that is a fantasy until the lycans are wiped from this earth forever, promise you will help us to do this and I will promise to support you in finding Nikolas and finding out who you truly are." She said, her words confused Faylan but she nodded "okay, I promise." She replied and Marla smiled and called in one of the guards to get them supplies and give their weapons back to them.

They were on the road again within an hour with a new direction and bags of food and clothes.

Faylan was quiet, Marla's words spinning around in her head

'Finding out who you truly are'

What had she meant? She was an Elf, that she knew. She liked women; she knew that too. She didn't know what else it could be. Eliana noticed her silence and looked at her "She was probably just talking about your sexuality and your feelings for me." She smiled and Faylan looked at her "What do you mean?"

"Oh, come on, it's obvious." Eliana laughed softly "It's cute" She gently bumped her shoulder and Faylan blushed and felt the points of her ears heat up from embarrassment, suddenly very grateful for her hair covering her ears "Sorry, I know you probably don't feel the same." She sighed, preparing herself for the rejection that she thought was inevitable but Eliana just took her hand in hers "I never said I didn't like you dummy" She gave her a cheeky grin, making Faylan giggle quietly, going shy with happiness as they followed the directions that Daria gave them. Faylan turned those words over in her mind, trying to figure out if she was joking or not. If she meant it then she would be over the moon but if she was joking, she honestly didn't know what she would do. She realised the reality that she might have to go home, she hated even the thought of that, being married to someone she didn't love and becoming, what the mortals would call, a housewife. She was horrified by that idea, pushing it from her mind. She did miss her father, though she doubted he'd be allowed to let her come back after she ran away, her mother would be furious and she was afraid of what her reaction would be. She wanted to be free and live a life of her own and her mother would never understand that.

She kept walking, a little faster now. Eliana noticed, catching up "In a hurry?" she playfully joked and Faylan nodded "he could be hurt or worse for all we know." She said, making her mind race with different possibilities and fears. He had become her best friend over the past few months and she hated the idea of losing him, of never hearing his laugh again, of never being able to have their deep conversations in the middle of the night over cups of tea when they can't sleep. It was the little things like that which made life worth living, worth fighting for.

They walked for what felt like years. Faylan didn't want to rest, she just wanted to find Nikolas, she wanted him back. However, the longer the journey took, the more anxious she became. They eventually came across a small village, wanting to find shelter for the night, and they walked toward it. Faylan was exhausted and she could tell that Eliana was too, she felt bad that she had made her keep walking. She had gone quiet a few hours earlier which is when she started to feel bad as she was tired and probably a little bit annoyed when she'd denied her a rest for any longer than 15 minutes. She looked at her, an apologetic smile on her face and Eliana looked at her and her face softened "I know you're worried about him but I'm sure he'll be okay for one night" she said gently and Faylan nodded "Yeah, I hope so" she smiled as they walked towards the inn. They got a room for the night, Faylan collapsed into the bed with a sigh, her legs suddenly feeling the pain from walking all day. She closed her eyes for a moment, feeling Eliana sit next to her on the bed "So you and Nikolas…" she started, making Faylan cringe a little on the inside, worried about what she was going to say "Do you like him?" she asked bluntly and Faylan opened her eyes "what? No, I mean he's a great friend, maybe even my best friend but I don't like him like that." She could almost feel the relief in Eliana when she said that, "Life has just become so much more complicated than it was a few months ago, I just don't think there's enough time to stop and think about that kind of stuff" Faylan explained, sitting up, looking at Eliana who nodded and smiled "I understand, maybe when all this is over, you can start to look for someone" she chuckled and Faylan smiled "yeah, maybe, if I survive this"

"You will, I won't let anything happen to you, I promise." She said gently but with a small tone of protectiveness in her voice. She loved how protective she was of her already, even though she didn't know her that well. She wanted to ask her why, why she wanted to keep her safe when she could easily turn her over to the lycans and be done with the whole thing, maybe even be seen as a hero to them but of course this would make her an enemy to the elves, it was a very complicated situation but she was glad she hadn't taken the easy way out of this mess. She looked at Eliana "Why do you want to protect me?" she asked, propping herself up on her elbows. Eliana sighed, crossing her legs underneath her "You're an innocent caught up in a war that isn't your fault. I feel a strong connection to you that I have never felt for anyone else in my ridiculously long life" She smiled at her "You make me feel more alive than I have in 500 years and I'm not just saying that I mean it" she said, her voice sincere, making Faylan blush, looking down at her hands nervously "I'm glad I do" she said shyly, looking at her through the hair that had fallen in front of her face. Eliana gently moved her hair out of her face, making Faylan blush a little deeper as she tucked it behind her ear, running her finger gently over the point, one of the only ways to tell she was an elf. She looked into Eliana's bright red eyes, there was a hint of danger and risk in what she was thinking but at the moment she didn't care. She wasn't going to waste this opportunity, one that may not come again. She slowly leaned in, allowing Eliana to move away but she didn't. She pressed her lips to hers; they were just as soft as she'd imagined. The kiss was gentle and soft, exactly how she had pictured it being. She was kissing Eliana Creighton and she never wanted it to end.

Chapter 9

She woke up the next morning, Eliana beside her, still asleep. She thought about the night before. The way she felt, she wondered if it had meant anything, if Eliana had just done it because she felt guilty. She shook her head, pushing that thought away, she would never do that to her...she didn't think. She sighed, sitting up, careful not to disturb Eliana. She looked over at her sleeping form, admiring her features. She loved how peaceful she looked when she slept, like she didn't have a care in the world, like the world wasn't about to change forever, either for the worse or the better depending on how the next few weeks went. She wanted so badly for this to be over, for the war to be done so that things could go back to normal, so she could get herself a nice place in the forest somewhere, a little cottage with fields of corn and vegetables that she would sell at the local market. She would have a dog or maybe even a wolf, she'd always wanted one, and she could see Eliana curled up in a chair with a book, and a teacup beside her. She smiled at the thought as she got up and made herself a tea. Her thoughts drifted to Nikolas as she stirred sugar into her tea. She wondered if he was okay and if he wasn't, that he was safe and being looked after. She knew this was wishful thinking if he was in the lycans possession. She knew that they would use whatever technique possible to get any sort of information out of him about the elves if he refused. Or didn't know anything? They would kill him. They would do it to send a message and as a threat to the entire world that they were willing to do whatever they could to get to the elves, to win this war.

Faylan was reading one of the books she'd taken from the witches about controlling her powers when Eliana woke up. She looked around and her eyes landed on Faylan and she smiled "Good morning" she chuckled and Faylan looked up at her "Morning"

"What is that you're reading?" She asked as she sat up, stretching. Faylan smiled "It's a book on how to control my powers, thought it might be useful so I don't accidentally hurt someone." She said seriously and Eliana nodded, understanding. She knew all too well what it was like to lose control and hurt someone, it stays with you forever. She got up and announced she was going to shower. She entered the bathroom, closing the door behind her and locking it. She leaned against the door, sighing deeply. She didn't know what to think about the night before. She didn't know whether Faylan was truly interested in her or just because of her looks. She had gotten that a lot in the past, people using her because of her looks and then throwing her away when they got bored or found someone better. Those events led to a lot of trust issues for Eliana, she was warier of people and didn't just give her heart out to anyone. She needed to know if Faylan was true. She could use her magic but she felt that was an invasion of privacy and would just lead to an argument and truths about her past that she didn't want outing.

She stepped into the shower, letting the warm water run over her aching body as she thought. This war could not end well. It won't. She knew that for sure. People were going to get hurt. People were going to die and regardless of who won it, it wouldn't be a celebration, it would be a funeral. That she knew for sure. And what would happen to Faylan? The war was already changing her, already making her ruthless and violent. She wasn't the same girl she'd met in the elf kingdom; she wasn't as happy or carefree. Her life had now become a fight for survival, living in fear for her friends and family. It upset Eliana to think, that that girl she had first met, was most likely gone, though slivers of her remained and she saw one last night. That is what she held on to, that is what was going to keep her going, the possibility that one day, she might see that girl again, the girl she caught feelings for.

After showering and changing, Eliana sat down on the bed, looking at the map and trying to figure out where to go next. She sighed in frustration, chewing on the end of her pencil. She was so focused on what she was doing, that she hardly noticed the bed sinking beside her as Faylan sat down "What are you thinking?" She asked and Eliana looked at her, 'You' was what she wanted to say but what came out was "How to find Nikolas and then get us back to the vampires in one piece, it's a little harder than it looks." She sighed and Faylan rested a hand on her shoulder "It's okay, you'll figure it out, you always do." She smiled kindly, a face that made Eliana swoon. She fought back the urge to kiss her, instead, she patted her hand "Thank you." She smiled back and put the map down, mentally giving up, she thought they might as well check out the other nest and go from there. She laid down on the bed, her mind slowly calming down. She closed her eyes and allowed her thoughts to drift. She thought of her family, her quickly dwindling coven, and the countless massacres of her kind. The future was looking pretty bleak for her kind, she had to admit. Her kind wanted nothing to do with this war, they were a peaceful race but there had to be a reason why they were being dragged into it, she just

didn't know what yet. Maybe
Nikolas had the answers, all the
more reason to find him. She
wanted to scream, why was
nothing easy when you needed it
to be? She just wanted to find
Nikolas and end this war so
everyone could go home and not
have to worry if they were going to
die tomorrow. She sighed and
opened her eyes, turning her head
to look up at Faylan who was
admiring her. Faylan quickly looked
away when she realised her eyes
were open, not able to hide the red
tint to her cheeks, however, from
being caught. Eliana smiled "It's
okay to look you know, I know I'm
very pretty." She joked and Faylan
chuckled lightly "You are." This
made Eliana blush, she had been
complimented on her looks before
but it was always because they
wanted something out of her but
the way Faylan said it, she truly
meant it with no other motives
other than to be nice. She looked

at her and sighed, coming to a
conclusion in her head about what
to do "I hate to do this since I am
so much more comfortable in here
than out there but I think, we
should keep going, and find
Nikolas." She said and Faylan
nodded slowly "Yeah, he could be
in trouble for all we know."

   "Or he could be completely fine,
you never know." Eliana said
reassuringly "Try to keep positive."
She smiled, her voice gentle,
reassuring Faylan that everything
was probably fine and she was just
overthinking things. That tended to
happen when she was worried, her
brain didn't quite think logically.
She got changed into her travelling
gear and started to pack
everything into her bag. Eliana
came over and gently put her hand
on her shoulder "It will all be over
soon, I promise, and then we can
go wherever you want and be
whatever you want." Her voice
trailed off shyly at the end and

Faylan smiled and gently placed a hand on top of hers "That sounds like a plan." She said gently. They gathered the rest of their belongings and left the room, not knowing that that was the last moment of happiness they'd have for a long time.

Chapter 10

It felt like weeks before they made it to the last vampire nest in the area. They were exhausted and were grumpy from lack of good sleep and good food. They entered the nest, Faylan's eyes moving from person to person as they walked past, they must have been made aware that they were coming because there was no security when they got there. Eliana started talking to the leader, he was a very tall man, at lead 6'7, and had long black hair and blood-red eyes which were staring intently down at her as she spoke. Faylan tuned out, looking around, desperately searching for Nikolas's face in the crowd, no such luck so far but there could be more vampires further in, she reminded herself, she had to stay positive even though it was slowly dwindling. She started to lose hope that she would ever see him again when she heard a familiar voice from behind her "Fay?" she whirled round, her face lighting up and her eyes welling up when she saw him "Nik!" She grinned and ran to him, hugging him tightly. He winced a little and she let go. She hadn't properly looked at him. His face was bruised and his left eye was swollen shut. He had multiple cuts on his face and his lip was split. As she had let go, she felt that his ribs might be broken. Why wasn't he healing? vampires were able to heal instantly "I know, sexy right?" Nikolas joked slightly and smiled a little before his lip restricted him "he was taken by the wolves and tortured for information. Information on you." The leader said, looking at Faylan with an accusatory look "Stop it father, it is not her fault." Nikolas said firmly and looked at her with a sad face "They killed them to get to me, my mother, and the girl I loved." His voice was sad, the memory clearly pained him. He straightened up after a moment "Forgive my father's rudeness, he seems to be lacking in manners since I got back."

"Only to the person who is clearly responsible for my wife's death." He scowled at Faylan. She wanted to sink into the floor and disappear. She backed away as Nikolas's father got closer to her "What do they want with you? huh? What is so special about you that they would kill my wife?"

"How the hell should I know?!" Faylan snapped, a sudden anger coming over her, he didn't get to talk to her like that, it didn't matter who he was "All I am is an elf princess, I don't know why they want me, and Eliana and I are trying to figure that out so don't you dare talk to me that way!" She hoisted her chin up like she used to, it was a way of showing her power, that she was better than everyone else. Nikolas smirked, enjoying his father's look of shock, embarrassment, and fury. He stormed off and Nikolas laughed lightly when he knew his father couldn't hear him "I have never seen anyone talk to him like that, except my mother, very impressive." He smiled and ruffled her hair. She let out a deep breath that she didn't realise she was holding in and went a little red "I don't know where that came from, I guess it's a mixture of tiredness and starvation." She chuckled lightly and Nikolas smiled "Let's get you fed then huh?" he led them through the nest, there were loads of rooms, some looked like armouries, some bedrooms, and some bathrooms. They finally came to the kitchen, it was big, a table with 10 chairs around it was in the centre of the room. Nikolas motioned for the people in the room to leave, once they were alone, he turned and looked at the girls "You guys look like hell, you have really been looking for me all this time?"

"Of course! why wouldn't we?" Faylan looked up at him and he chuckled "Because I'm dead weight Fay, you know it. Eliana knows it too, my people have told her as much, haven't they." He looked at Eliana who sighed and looked at him sadly "They don't look too kindly on you; I will admit but that's just because you and Faylan refused to bind the two species together and form a very powerful alliance."

"It wouldn't have been right and you know it." He said as he turned around, getting some food from the cupboards to cook for them. He started to cut up vegetables "We didn't start this war, the lycans did, we all just, unfortunately, got caught up in it." He said, his voice flat and almost emotionless. He turned round to face the girls

"Look, we can all get through this if we work together and don't turn on each other, a notion that my father clearly hasn't mastered yet." He sighed, Faylan could tell he was clearly hurting a lot but trying to mask it behind focus and determination to win the war. For his mother and his girlfriend. She went the place a hand on his shoulder but drew her hand back, an odd feeling coming over her, telling her not to do it. She instead leaned against the counter "I know this situation isn't ideal…" he looked at her when she said this, his face an expression of incredulity "Isn't ideal?" he scoffed "The world is falling apart, entire covens and nests are being wiped off the map, but god forbid it ruins your day princess." He snapped, putting the vegetables into the pan and starting on the meat. Faylan looked at him with hurt and anger before leaving the room "What happened to you, Nikolas? That was completely uncalled for, you know this isn't her fault." Eliana glared at him, crossing her arms. Nikolas sighed "I never wanted to upset her but I can't ignore what the lycans told me about her."

"They are liars and you know it, they will say anything to sway people to join their side." She snapped angrily and stalked out of the room, Nikolas hung his head, feeling terrible for what he said but he didn't follow them.

****

Faylan wandered through the nest, eventually finding a huge library, she slipped inside and closed the door. She'd hide in here for a while, read a book, and try to forget the last few minutes. She didn't know what had got into Nikolas but she knew he wasn't himself; he couldn't be. He would never snap at her like that. She found an old and battered copy of Jekyll and Hyde and sat down in an armchair. She tried to theorise why he would have spoken to her like that, eventually going with the fact that the lycans tortured him. She sighed deeply and curled up, reading the book for a while before she heard the door open. She looked up from the book and saw Eliana, she smiled gently at her "Found a good book I see." She chuckled lightly as Faylan closed the book "I know you're checking on me, I'm fine, really." She lied and Eliana pulled up another chair and sat down next to her "I know that's not true love." She said gently and Faylan sighed "he didn't mean what he said, the wolves just got into his head and with everything that's happened to him, he just snapped."

"I'm just a reminder of what happened to his mother and girlfriend." Faylan said, "Maybe coming here was a mistake, maybe we should just go back to the elves, and wait for the war to be over." Her voice was tired, and aged. It was like the war had aged her massively in just a few months. Eliana looked at her with sad eyes "I know this war has taken something from all of us and we all want it to end but splitting up now won't help, it will make things worse. We all need to be united to take down the lycans." Faylan knew she was right and hated it, she just wanted everything to go back to the way it was.

She put the book down and looked at her "Can I try something?" she asked, looking and Eliana who nodded "Okay, sure." She smiled gently and Faylan moved closer to her, they were close enough now that she could feel her breath on her face. Eliana bit her lip for a moment before Faylan gently cupped her face and kissed her gently. She smelled of leather and tasted of something sweet. The kiss started off gentle and slow but quickly got heated and fierce. She tangled her hands through her hair and Eliana gently gripped her waist, her hands sneaking under her shirt a little. Faylan shivered at her touch, tightening her grip on her hair and before she knew it, she was pulled onto Eliana's lap, the kiss becoming more intense. They jumped and pulled apart when they heard the door open "Fayl-" Nikolas's voice cut off when he saw them, he cleared his throat "Sorry, just...food is ready" he said awkwardly as he quickly left the room. As soon as the door closed, they burst into laughter, Faylan looking into Eliana's eyes "Let's hold this thought" she giggled "and go get something to eat."

"Well, I am going to need my stamina, and so will you." She playfully winked at her, grinning when she went bright red as she got up. Eliana got up and took her hand, leading her back to the kitchen, Faylan still bright red and

excited for what the rest of the
night held.

Chapter 11

Eliana wandered down to the kitchen the next morning and made a pot of coffee. She leaned against the counter as she waited for it to boil, she thought about the night before and couldn't help but smile. She closed her eyes, her body remembering the feel of her lips on her skin, making her body shiver. She felt herself blush and squeak when she heard footsteps coming down the corridor and quickly went back to making the coffee. Nikolas entered the room "Morning" he said and stopped short when he saw her "Had some fun last night did we?" he smirked, she looked at him, confused as to how he would know that but he pointed to her neck and smiled, she quickly looked in her reflection and went red when she noticed that her neck was littered with love bites. She gasped and quickly covered her neck, making Nikolas chuckle "Follow me, I'll help." he took her hand and led her to his room where his girlfriend's makeup still sat. He sat her down on a chair and grabbed some things to cover her neck with. They sat in silence for a moment as he applied the makeup to her neck before he said "I'm sorry for snapping at you yesterday, it wasn't fair."

"It's okay." She said softly "You've been under a lot of stress recently."

"That is not an excuse for my behaviour." He said, looking at her "I shouldn't have been so harsh." He sighed and she gently took his hand "It's okay, I forgive you." She smiled at him and he continued to apply the makeup "So, do you want to talk about this." He smirked and she blushed, gently hitting his leg "Shut up."

"I'm happy for you, it's what you've wanted for ages. Are you together?"

"I don't know." She said, looking down "I don't want this to be some one-night stand and go no further, I want something with her, a future." She admitted, looking at him. He smiled and placed a hand on top of hers "Tell her that, talk to her." He reassured, "I am sure she feels the same, it's pretty obvious that she does." He chuckled lightly and she smiled, thinking as he finished covering her neck, did she really like her? She hoped so, she didn't know what she would do if she got turned down. Would she just go home? Would she stay here and try and move forward from it? Could she do that? She wanted to believe she could but in reality, she wasn't so sure. After a few moments of chatting and slight pain from where Nikolas was applying the makeup, her neck was all covered. She looked at herself in the mirror and smiled "Thanks Nik, I look much better" she chuckled lightly and he smiled, putting the makeup kit down "Now, go talk to her, I'll meet you in the war room when you're ready." He smiled at her and got up, leaving the room. She sighed, looking at herself in the mirror, psyching herself up for what she knew could be a very uncomfortable conversation if it went the wrong way. She tried not to think negatively as she walked back to her room. She entered the room and found Eliana sitting up and reading a book "Morning." She smiled and Faylan sat down beside her "Do you want to be with me?" she asked bluntly and Eliana made a noise of surprise "Straight to the point eh." She chuckled nervously and cleared her throat as she set the book down, turning to face her completely, the sun shining off her face, making her look even more angelic than Faylan already thought she looked. She took a deep breath and sighed "The answer to your question is…yes,

yes I do." She smiled at her, chuckling a little at the worry on her face when she paused. It earned her a gentle smack on the leg "Don't scare me like that." Faylan sighed and looked at her "You want to be with me? Really?"

"Yes, you idiot." She teased and laughed cutely when she was tackled in a hug, landing with Faylan on top of her, she tucked a stray bit of hair behind her ear as she looked up at her. Faylan looked down at her with a smile and leaned down, gently kissing her. They kissed for a moment before she pulled back and looked at her "Where do we go from here?"

"Well, first we have to win this war and then we find somewhere quiet and peaceful and go on with our lives, figure us out and what we want to do from there." Eliana smiled up at her and Faylan blushed and grinned "Sounds like a plan." She giggled.

They spent the day planning
what to do. Faylan was slowly
getting more and more fed up with
the leader, his ideas were so
unhelpful. She eventually snapped
"I suppose you just want to get us
all killed then!" she half shouted
and the room fell silent. Nikolas
tried to hide his laugh with a
cough. The leader shot her a
hateful glare "If you're so smart,
you figure it out then" he snarled
and she stood up straighter and
looked over the plans, pointing out
the best one "This one will work
best, if we can get the elves to
cooperate with us and the witches,
we will have the wolves
outnumbered" she explained,
Nikolas looked at her with an
impressed expression on his face.
The rest of the room suddenly
recovered from her outburst a
moment earlier and started giving
their opinions and support of the
idea "You'll need to arrange a
meeting with your parents, I can

get my people there" Eliana said, placing a hand on her shoulder, knowing this was going to be a daunting task for her. Faylan knew her parents weren't going to like this but it was their best option. She looked at Nikolas "Travel with me?" He nodded and she looked at Eliana "Get your leaders to the elf kingdom, I'll meet you there" She gently placed a hand on her cheek before swiftly leaving the room, Nikolas close behind.

Chapter 12

The journey back to her home was a long and tiring one, especially painful since they spent hours on a horse. She dreaded having to face her parents after she ran away. She dreaded what her mother would say "It'll be okay Fay, just stand your ground and take no prisoners, like you did in the war room" Nikolas comforted, placing a hand on top of hers and snapping her out of her thoughts. She smiled and nodded, this was how it had to be if they wanted any chance of winning this war because, by the sounds of it, the Lycans were quickly getting the upper hand.

Once they got there, they were led through to the main hall. She had never seen the entrance from a visitor's perspective, nor had she been treated like a visitor before. It was definitely a weird situation but then again, the whole world was going up in flames so a little weird was nice compared to the fear she had felt for the last few uncertain months. They reached the main hall and she looked up at her parents, sitting on their thrones "Well, you're alive" her mother's voice was full of venom and anger, ignoring her husband's attempts to calm her with a hand to her arm "why have you come back here?"

"The world is at war and we need an alliance between elves, vampires, and witches in order to win" Nikolas spoke up, his voice calm and firm. Faylan's mother scoffed but her husband put his hand up to silence her "Quiet, let's hear what they have to say"

"Darling-"

"Enough, our daughter is back, alive and with a plan to win us the war, the least we can do is listen to her unless you want to continue being spiteful and kill us all?" he retorted, angrily, making Faylan smile a little as her mother shut her mouth in defeat and got up, storming out of the room. Faylan watched her leave, her heart breaking a little before her father said "Go ahead my love, what did you have in mind?" his voice was gentle and she looked at him and smiled. She spent the next few moments going over their plan from start to finish, her father nodded along with what she was saying.

When she was done her father looked at her with a proud look on his face "How much you have grown" he stood up and walked over to her, gently cupping her face "So strong and beautiful" he smiled "The elves will join you, regardless of what your mother says" he playfully winked at her and she grinned, hugging him tightly "it is so good to see you again papa"

"Same to you my love" he held her tightly, kissing the top of her head "You are a warrior now by the looks of things, you look just like him" he smiled sadly and Faylan's breath shuddered "he was meant to marry too but he found himself in the battlefield, he wanted to fight, not rule, seems you followed in his footsteps" her father smiled, gently pulling away so he could look at her "your brother would be so proud of you, just as I am" Faylan smiled happily, her eyes watering a little. They never talked about him but it was really nice, to talk about him in a normal way, not just denying his existence like her mother did.

She spent the afternoon walking the grounds with her father, talking and laughing. She'd missed this, quality time with her father, the way they used to before the world and their lives became so complicated and messed up. She took a deep breath and looked at her father "I'm with her papa, the witch that came to tell us about the lycans to begin with" Her father chuckled "I knew there was something else that was different about you" he smiled "Are you happy?"

"I am, really happy" She couldn't help but smile wide at the thought of Eliana and her father took her hand in his "Then I am happy for you my love, for whatever you decide in the future, you have my blessing." His voice was genuine and full of love as he spoke. Faylan nodded, smiling happily "Thank you papa." She couldn't express the complete amount of gratitude she had for her father and his continuing acceptance of everything she was and wanted to be. She knew her mother would never accept her so she decided then and there to never tell her, even if that meant never seeing her again. She didn't want to lose her father though; she knew that he would end up in the middle and he would be the collateral damage if she never saw her mother again and she didn't know if she could do that to him.

She sighed deeply, looking out at the fountains, bringing back the memories of her first conversation with Eliana and how far they had come since then. How far she had come, how much she had grown. She barely recognised the girl she used to be and she never wanted to be that girl again. She looked over at the forest, noticing little twinkles in the trees "Someone must have put up windchimes" she thought out loud, her father looking at them before grabbing her arm, and pulling her up "Those aren't windchimes Fay, they're lights" his voice was fast, scared as he quickly pulled her towards the greenhouse. She looked back, her heart filling with fear as she realised there were lycans charging them. The guards ran past them, trying to fend them off, their grunts and screams of pain ringing in her ears as she was pushed inside, her father closing the doors with him on the other side "Go my love, quickly now, I will buy you some time."

"No!" she screamed "Papa, please! No!" he put his hand on the glass and she put hers in the same place, trying to touch him through the glass, though she knew it was impossible "I love you Faylan" he said before getting his sword out, walking away towards the horde of lycans. Faylan screamed for him and continued to as Nikolas carried her away. The screaming of the guards and the rest of the elves consumed them as they made their way out of the kingdom. They made it to their horse, making their getaway. Lycans ran after them, they were incredibly fast in their wolf form. They stayed ahead of them for a while before one scratched at the horse with its claws, sending them flying off. Faylan grunted as she landed, the wind knocked out of her and her ears ringing. She felt the back of her head and felt blood, she'd hit it when she fell "Nikolas?" she groaned, looking up at the looming figure above her "Think again Princess" the familiar voice of a lycan general came through the fuzziness of her ears…Darion…

Chapter 13

Faylan had lost track of the amount of time she had spent on the road. Her hands were bound and she was gagged for most of the time unless she was eating or drinking. She had no idea what had happened to Nikolas, the last she saw of him, he was lying on the floor, unconscious. She'd been grabbed and shoved onto a horse, looking back she saw her home go up in flames and the distant screaming could barely be heard over the cheering of the lycans. She had been sat down on the ground when they stopped for the night, her thoughts consuming her while everyone else was crowding around a fire, eating "too much to think about?" Darion sat beside her, offering her some of his food. She turned her head away and said "Leave me alone"

"Look, I'm sorry about your parents," he said, his tone

strangely gentle, making her scoff "I am but in war, there will always be collateral damage," he said and she glared at him "collateral damage?! My parents are not just collateral damage!" she half shouted and he sighed "you're right but they started this war, not me, actions always have consequences or did they not teach you that."

"They taught me how to be a good person, clearly something your parents didn't teach you cause you're an ass" she spat and he narrowed his eyes at her "I know you are angry but you don't talk about my parents like that, you may be a princess where you come from but with us, you're just another elf" he growled, getting up and storming off, leaving her alone with her thoughts again. She thought about her parents, and how her father sacrificed himself for her. She hated him for that, why couldn't he have just left with her? Why did he have to be a hero? She looked out into the forest as she started to tear up, she refused to let anyone see her cry, even if they weren't paying attention to her. Assuming she was the new queen, she had to be strong, powerful and crying would just be seen as weakness and Faylan refused to be weak. She thought about Nikolas and Eliana, where were they? Were they okay? Were they even alive? She hoped so, she needed them to be, how else was she going to get rescued, if they even knew she was alive. She wondered what would happen if they thought she was dead, would they keep fighting? Would they turn her and her family into martyrs and use them to bring everyone together? She hoped so, even if she wasn't found, she would still be doing something towards them winning the war. Darion came back over a while later, sitting back down next to her, placing a fresh plate of food in front of her "Please eat something, I can't have you starving to death on my watch" his voice almost resembled someone who cared. Her hunger was the only reason she took the food and started to eat. He looked at her "What do you know about your family?" he asked, his question taking her off guard "I don't know what you mean" she replied, her mouth filled with food as she placed the plate down. Dario chuckled lightly "I mean how well do you know them? Your brother specifically."

"Don't talk about my brother"

"I don't mean to upset you, I am merely curious, we have been told one story and I simply want to hear what your parents told you," He said, his voice genuine and she sighed "I was told that he was murdered by a lycan and that's what started the war," she said and he sucked in a breath "that is

not what we were told, well not
completely anyways. We were told
that he killed one of ours, for
seemingly no reason but to start a
war because that is the only way
he saw to get out of a forced
marriage and so our people
retaliated and killed him, hoping it
would end there but it didn't." he
explained and Faylan looked at him
"is that true?" she asked and he
nodded "it is, I spoke to the family
of the lycan he killed and they
confirmed it" he sounded almost
sorry to be telling her all of this.
She couldn't believe it, her brother
was a killer, he killed an innocent
just to get out of a marriage and
ended up starting a war "what an
idiot" she said aloud "my brother I
mean, I don't understand why he
couldn't just run away like I did,
killing should never have been the
answer" she sighed and Darion
looked at her "I am sorry that you
had to hear all of that from me but
I was just curious to see if you

were fighting us with the truth or lies"

"No, it's okay, thank you" she said softly "I can't believe I'm saying that but I mean it"

"It's alright, we're not the only lycan and elf to get along, I heard a rumour that there was a child of both our species out there somewhere and that they had the power to bring our species together or to destroy us completely, depending on which species is telling the story" He chuckled lightly and Faylan thought for a moment, what if he was right? Maybe this child could save them all, maybe it could stop the war "we need to find this child," she said eventually and he looked at her "are you sure?"

"Yes, if they can stop this war and the people, I love from dying, then we need to find the child," she said and he nodded "Okay, though you may not like what you find," he said before standing up and walking off before she could respond. He knew something, she could sense it and she would find out, no matter the cost.

Chapter 14

Faylan spent the next few weeks with the lycans, she and Darion even became acquaintances, though she didn't completely trust him. He could have been completely lying about what he said in an attempt to make her trust him, she wasn't sure what the purpose for that would be though. The rest of the group, or pack as Darion called them, didn't like her and they made it very clear with the little food and water they gave her and the little punches and kicks they landed as they passed her. At first it hurt her but eventually she just became numb to it. She kept her stare straight ahead, ignoring them. Eventually they gave up when she gave them no response to their actions, clearly it had become boring to them.

She shifted her fingers; the tightness of the ropes had made it so her hands were slowly losing feeling. She grumbled a little as she started getting pins and needles in her fingers as she moved them. She'd been sat on the ground and in such an uncomfortable position for so long that her whole body was stiff. She cracked her neck first and then her back, sighing with relief. She moved her legs around to avoid pins and needles there too. "I know it's uncomfortable" Darion said as he moved to sit next to her "but it's the best we got"

"Well, the least you could do would be to allow me to get up and walk around for a bit, I can barely feel half my body." She grumbled, fed up with all the constant moving camps and unfair treatment. He gave her an apologetic look but she ignored it and focused on moving her body around. After a few moments of silence, Darion got up, walking away when an arrow whistled past his head. He immediately turned around as another lodged in his shoulder. Suddenly, a mass of arrows unleashed on the camp, Faylan flung herself to the floor, covering her head with her arms. The shouts and arrows landing ended after a few moments and she peaked up. The entire camp as covered in arrows and bodies; everyone was dead though she couldn't see Darion's body anywhere. She felt the ties on her hands being cut and she looked up, seeing Nikolas squatting beside her. She let out a small noise of happiness and flung her arms around him "I thought you were dead!"

"So did I" he said and showed her the wound on his chest. It was a very deep gash that had been crudely stitched up and was slowly starting to heal. She looked at him as he helped her up, the efforts to prevent pins and needles in her feet had failed as she slightly collapsed into him, small pinches of pain shooting through her feet "you, okay?" he asked, concerned as he held her up. She nodded "pins and needles, been sat down for god knows how long" she sighed. They stayed there for a while until she could walk normally again. She moved away and cracked her back and neck loudly, sighing in relief "how did you find me?" she asked eventually "we've been tracking them for weeks, trying to figure out where they were going, their plans and such"

"So, you had weeks to rescue me but you chose not to?" She looked up at him accusingly and he sighed "Fay, we needed to figure out what their plans were, we couldn't risk losing that chance" he explained and she scoffed and walked away from him just as another vampire dragged Darion over to Nikolas. He was battered, bruised and bleeding, gripping his shoulder where the arrow had hit. Nikolas looked at him "tie him up,

we can get information out of him"
he ordered and the vampire tied
him up and took him away.

~~~~~~~~~~~~~

They spent the next few days
making their way back to Faylan's
kingdom. She had no idea what to
expect, she didn't even know if her
home would be still standing. She
wondered if she'd find her father
there, or his body at least and she
could give him a proper burial.
Maybe she'd find out what
happened to her mother, whether
she was alive or dead or missing.
She sighed, looking at the floor as
she walked. They only had a few
hours left until they made it and
she was trying to prepare herself
for anything.

The castle looked mostly intact,
there were a few holes where parts
of walls had been blown out. She
was almost surprised that there
were no bodies as she walked
through the building. She entered

the main hall and looked at the thrones at the other end of the room. Her fathers had been completely destroyed, there was some sad symbolism in that, it almost confirmed to her that he was dead even though she knew it. She broke away from the group and headed for the greenhouse, the place she last saw her father. Maybe she hoped to find his body so she could bury him but a part of her didn't want to see whatever condition he was in. She knew she would never be able to unsee it if he was in bad condition.

She walked out the glass doors and toward the fountain. There were still a few bodies on the floor, they were guards by the looks of their armour *why didn't anyone bury them?'* she thought, they were just as important as anyone else and deserved the same treatment of respect. She kept walking, there were bodies of elves and lycans scattered around. She

eventually found her father. Her
breath caught in her throat; he had
been ripped apart. She sat down
next to him, unable to process
what she was seeing and how to
think. She placed a hand on his
head, his lifeless eye looking up at
the sky, she carefully closed his
eyes and started to cry. She hung
her head, placing her forehead on
his and sobbed. Memories of her
father flashed through her mind,
making her sob even harder. She
barely noticed Nikolas coming up
beside her, placing a hand on her
shoulder to comfort her. He gently
rubbed her shoulder, not saying
anything, which she really
appreciated. She didn't know how
she would handle it if he gave her
pity, she didn't want pity.

Eventually she stopped crying
and said "we need to bury him"
she sniffled and Nikolas nodded
"however you want it done darling"
he said gently and she slowly stood
up, her legs shaking a little as she

stumbled to the nearby bench, collapsing onto it. She watched as Nikolas and a couple of others dug a hole and helped to pick him up to carefully place him in the hole once they'd wrapped him in a sheet. She looked down at her hands, she hadn't noticed by they were covered in blood. Nikolas came over after a few moments and saw her hands "let's get you cleaned up, okay?" he said gently, taking her hands and leading her back inside and to the bathroom, gently washing her hands for her.

She spent the next few days in bed, she barely spoke or ate. Nikolas made her food but it ended up discarded on her nightstand. She didn't know how to process her father's death, especially not with what she had seen. Thoughts of finding her mother were completely forgotten. She felt numb, unable to move as if she was paralysed from the neck down. Nikolas came in a few times a day to give her updates on what was happening with Darion and that he had sent Eliana out to try and find her mother or any information on where she had gone or if she was dead. He never got any response from Faylan though so after about 10 minutes, he would leave again and she would be alone with her thoughts. Her happy memories of her father were now tainted by his death and her finding his body.

She curled up in bed, closing her eyes. She hadn't slept properly in days, every time she tried to, she would be plagued with nightmares that left her screaming and crying and in worst case, paralysed with fear for a minute or two before finally being able to move and scream. Nikolas came in every time she woke up screaming and held her until she fell back to sleep. It got to the point where he would simply sleep on a chair in her room so he would be there when she needed him, the nightmares happened every night and didn't get any better. By the end of the week, Nikolas looked almost as tired as she did. She felt awful for it but she didn't know how to tell him.

~~~~~~~~~~

2 weeks later Eliana came back. She knocked on her bedroom door and came in "hey, it's me, how are you doing?" she asked, sitting on the edge of Faylan's bed. Faylan turned over and looked at her, her eyes still dull and lifeless. Eliana ran her fingers through her hair "I'm so sorry, I know this hurts but I want to help you, how can I help?" she asked, her voice genuine and pleading as Faylan looked up at her "just…just stay with me" she croaked and Eliana tried to hide her surprise when she heard her talk but just nodded and laid down on the bed next to her. Faylan instinctively moved closer to her, wrapping her arms round her.

Eliana held her close "I'm going to be right here till you're feeling better, okay?" she said gently and Faylan nodded, slowly starting to feel more in touch with reality, Eliana just seemed to have that effect on her. She closed her eyes for a moment, trying to clear her mind of all the bad thoughts and get a peaceful sleep, she knew it was wishful thinking though. She didn't sleep these days, she didn't want to keep seeing the corpse of her father, didn't want to hear it talking to her, cursing her out and blaming her for his death. She squeezed her eyes shut, trying to hide from the images by burying her face in Eliana's shoulder and without even realising it, she fell asleep.

Chapter 15

She awoke almost a day later, Eliana was still next to her, one arm round her and the other holding a book. She was so engrossed in the book that she didn't notice her waking up. Faylan just looked at her for a few moments, wishing she could be like her old self again. She hated the feeling of numbness inside her, the lack of energy to do anything. She felt rested after her first peaceful sleep in weeks but somehow, she was still tired and as though she couldn't find the energy to even move to sit up. Eliana looked at her "oh hey, you're awake" she smiled "did you sleep okay?" she asked and for once Faylan could nod, she had slept like a baby, with no nightmares for once. "Anything about my mother?" she asked nervously and Eliana sighed softly and shook her head "nothing yet, but at least there's nothing definitively saying she's dead" she said, in an attempt to comfort her. Faylan nodded a little '*I suppose that is a positive*' she thought, trying not to let her mind wander to bad places. "I know this is a really bad time to ask…" Eliana approached whatever she was about to say carefully "but what do you want to do now? About the plan" she asked and Faylan sighed "well, I suppose I'm in charge now huh?" she said, her voice sad "keep to the plan, nothing changes" she nodded, trying to sound strong. Eliana picked up on this "you don't have to do this you know; I can take your place till you're feeling up to it"

"It's okay, I have to do this…for my father" Faylan said softly, as though mentioning him made her heart hurt. It did of course but she knew that she couldn't just never talk about him again, she needed to make him proud, needed to make his death mean something.

She eventually got up and headed to the bathroom, stripping off her clothes once she got there and stepped into the shower, turning it on. She let the warm water wash over her, shivering as a feeling of relaxation came over her. She felt her muscles relax and her mind go blank. She tilted her head up, letting the water run over her face as she sighed deeply, enjoying the warmth of the water.

She came out a few minutes later and got changed into her usual black leather pants and jacket with a lace top underneath. She looked at Eliana, who had put her book down once she'd come out "you sure about this?" Eliana asked and Faylan nodded "I think so"

"Well, I'll be right there beside you" she said gently, walking over to her and taking her hand in hers. Faylan smiled a little at her and started the walk down to the war room. She pushed open the doors and everyone went quiet, looking at her. Her heart started beating quicker as she suddenly felt very exposed with everyone looking at her "come on now folks, it's rude to stare" Nikolas's voice piped up from the other side of the room, giving Faylan an encouraging smile, showing her, he was happy to have her back. She smiled lightly back and moved towards the table, her hand still firmly clasped in Eliana's as she looked over the maps and the pieces on it. She gathered that the lycans had moved forward significantly and a few other small villages and kingdoms had fallen as there were pieces discarded on the table beside the map. She sighed softly "well this all looks awful" she half joked, earning a couple of looks from the others in the room. Nikolas chuckled "yeah, it is" he crossed the room and stood on the other side of her "we might need a new plan, a better one. We need to be more inconspicuous, more deadly" he said, looking at the map "any ideas?" he asked, looking at her and she shrugged "maybe more use of magic rather than brute force. The lycans use brute force, we need to be more imaginative than that so maybe using our magic and abilities might give us an advantage" she suggested, earning a few nods and noises of approval from a few in the room. Nikolas nodded "that could work, some of us will need training, to make sure we're using our power the best way we can, to do the most damage" he said and she nodded "you can use the guards old training room and the garden"

"What about you?" he asked "well, I will be coming to a few training sessions but I want to focus on finding my mother, she might be able to help, if she'd still alive" Faylan responded and

Nikolas nodded "we might have an update on that" he said "a woman was spotted in one of the other elf kingdoms who looked like your mother, her hair and clothes were different but she looked too much like her for us to ignore" he said and she looked at him "we need to go and get her, now! She could be in danger, she is the queen, she'll be used as leverage to make us all surrender" Faylan said and Nikolas placed a hand on her shoulder "calm down, I've sent some people out to bring her back, they should be back by tomorrow; okay?" he said gently and she nodded, looking at the map "okay, then we start training" she looked at Eliana "can you train the witches?" she asked and Eliana nodded "I'll train the elves and Nikolas can train the vampires" she looked at them both and he nodded "alright then; let's get to work" he chuckled, letting Faylan lead them both to the

training room. This was going to be
a long day.

Chapter 16

After hours of training, Faylan collapsed onto the chair in the greenhouse. She had always loved to sit in there when she just needed to clear her mind. The smell of the flowers helped to calm her down and relax her. She looked out the window, noticing that there was now a headstone where her father was buried "I put that up" Nikolas said, coming over to her side "I thought he deserved it" he looked at her and she smiled up at him "thank you" she looked out at the garden "the flowers are starting to bloom again, papa always loved flowers, looking after them and admiring his work once they'd bloomed" she smiled lightly "he always said when you take time to love and care for something, it always turns into something beautiful" she sighed and Nikolas looked down at her "I know you miss him but I know you'll make him proud with what you're doing" he said gently and she nodded "I know, I just wish he was here to guide me, he always knew just what to say and he had more experience in wars than I do" she chuckled lightly and Nikolas gently squeezed her shoulder "I think you're going an amazing job" his voice was genuine and serious as she looked up at him and gently patted his hand that was on her shoulder "thank you Nik, I am glad that I have you and Eliana by my side through this, I don't know what I would do without either of you" she said honestly and he smiled "I'm here till the end, no matter what happens" he smiled and looked at the door when he heard footsteps. There was a vampire in the doorway "sorry to interrupt but they're back" her voice was a little too high pitched for the gothic, bad girl look that she was sporting but Nikolas nodded "we're coming" he said and she gave a single nod and left the room "ready to see dear old mother?" he looked at Faylan who shrugged "honestly, I don't know but we'll find out" she chuckled lightly, getting up and following Nikolas to the main hall. She was oddly nervous, it was just her mother, though she had no idea how she was going to react to seeing her again, would she blame her for her father's death? Would she scream and shout at her? Or would she just be happy to know she was alive? She had no idea and she looked at the woman who had her back to her. Her hair was a deep red and her clothes were very similar to Faylans', they hugged her curves and looked almost a little too tight for her. She had never seen her mother out of very fancy and over the top dresses, they were always to show off her power and wealth to anyone who laid their eyes on her. Faylan had always hated those dresses, they just made her mother look narcissistic and as though all she every care about was money and power, though she supposed this wasn't completely untrue.

The woman turned around and it was indeed her mother. She held in the childlike urge to run to her and hug her, she kept up the appearance of being in charge, letting her mother come to her. Her mother made her way to her, her eyes filling with tears "My daughter, you're alive" she stated, her voice cracking a little from relief and happiness. Faylan nodded "father wasn't so lucky" she said sadly, her mother's face dropping and a choked sob came out of her mouth "oh god, I thought so when he hadn't come to find me" she sighed and looked at Faylan "how?"

"He saved my life, helping me escape" she said quietly, almost afraid of her reaction but her mother just nodded "he always did need to be the hero and he would never have let you get hurt, he would have died first" she said and then gasped when she realised what she had said but Faylan refused to show any sign of surprise. Her mother looked at her "no hug for your mother?" she said and Faylan scoffed "hug? After everything you have put me through?!" she laughed dryly and her mother sighed "I know I haven't always been the most supportive of you"

"Not the most supportive?! I had to run away because I was being forced into a marriage that I very clearly didn't want to and because I knew for a fact you would never accept the fact that I like girls" she said, folding her arms and giving her mother an accusatory stare, making her mother go a little red with embarrassment. She stammered, trying to come up with some sort of excuse but sighed in

defeat "I'm sorry" she simply said
and Faylan sighed "this isn't
important right now, we have a
war to win and then we can sort
out our family issues" she looked
at Nikolas "could you show my
mother to her room and inform her
of what's happening?" she asked
and Nikolas nodded "of course,
you're the boss" he smiled and
ushered her mother upstairs.
Eliana came into the room as
Faylan sat on the steps "family
reunion went that well?" she said
as she sat next to her and Faylan
laughed sarcastically "oh yeah,
we're going dancing in the flower
garden later" she joked and Eliana
took her hand "I'm here for you,
just remember that, and that you
are in charge here, not her, this is
your plan" she said reassuringly
and Faylan brought her hand up to
her lips and placed a soft kiss on it
"thank you, I mean that" she
smiled and rested her head on her
shoulder "our lives are so

complicated huh?" Faylan mumbled and Eliana giggled "oh yeah, I wouldn't have it any other way though. It brought us together, didn't it?" she always had a way of looking on the bright side, even when Faylan wasn't even sure there was one. She smiled softly, completely agreeing with her.

She enjoyed sitting there in silence with her for a little while, their silences were comfortable, never awkward and she loved them. She knew this war was going to take a lot from them, it had already taken almost everything from Faylan and she wasn't sure how much more loss she could take before completely breaking. She thought about this for a while before pushing the thoughts away. She needed to think more positively, or at least try to. She still had Nikolas and Eliana, she knew that with them by her side, she would be okay. She needed to stay positive, stay strong. She was slowly starting to feel a little bit less numb for the first time in weeks and she didn't want to lose that.

   She looked at Eliana "can we go to bed? I'm exhausted" she said, holding back a yawn and Eliana chuckled "alright, let's go" she got up and took Faylan to her room, laying down beside her. Faylan almost instantly fell asleep but Eliana stayed awake for a while, reading and then just looking at her for a bit.

Chapter 17

Faylan woke up in the middle of the night to hushed voices outside her door. She carefully got up, making sure not to wake up Eliana as she crept to the door, pressing her ear against it. She heard her mother's voice and another she didn't recognise and they seemed to be arguing about something. She didn't hear the whole conversation but she heard most of it "should we tell her?" the other voice said and her mother sighed "no, we can't, it would break her"

"She deserves to know" the other voice hissed, his voice irritated "no she doesn't, she loved her father, she doesn't need to know what he did" her mother hissed back quietly. What did her father do? Why was her mother so worried about her finding out? She was so confused but kept quiet, hoping they would say her father did "she deserves to know that her father was unfaithful" the voice hissed, Faylan let out a quiet gasp, her knees buckling and she hit the door, trying to regain balance "what was that?" her mother's voice said and Faylan quickly got back into bed and pretended to be asleep. The door creaked open a moment later, her heart pounding as she pretended to be asleep "she doesn't need to know" her mother said quietly and the door shut. She waited a minute before sitting up, trying to wrap her head around what she had heard, her father was unfaithful to her mother, how could she not have known this? Why didn't he tell her? Did her brother know? How long ago was it? How long did it go on for? So many questions filled her brain as she laid down and tried to get back to sleep. She was going to get answers from her mother tomorrow, she needed to know more. She closed her eyes and moved closer to Eliana, who draped an arm round her in her sleep and tried to fall asleep. She would find out more in the morning and why it was so bad that her mother had to hide it from her even after his death.

~~~~~~~~~~~~

  She woke up late the next day and felt the bed next to her, it was empty, Eliana was already awake. She sat up, remember what she had heard the night before, half wondering if it was just a very vivid dream, she hoped so. She got dressed into the same outfit as the day before and went down to the kitchen to find something to eat. She made something and started eating as Nikolas came in "morning sleepyhead" he chuckled and she playfully rolled her eyes at him "didn't sleep well last night" she mumbled behind the food in her mouth and he looked at her "nightmares again?"

"No, just couldn't get to sleep" she shrugged and kept eating, feeling bad for lying to him but she wanted answers first before she told him anything. He nodded "okay, well Eliana took over for you this morning with your people so they're ready for you whenever you are" he smiled and she sighed, already regretting the idea of training, she forgot just how intense and tiring training was all day, every day. She told him she'd be there in a bit and he left after getting a glass of water. She continued eating, thinking about what her mother was so afraid of her knowing, her father slept with someone else, it hurt her but she wasn't exactly surprised with how her mother used to treat him, but what if there was something more to it? Something big, what if her brother wasn't her mothers'? she pushed that thought aside, they would have told her if that was the case, although they never really talked about Taeral so it could be possible. What if she wasn't her mothers'? It would definitely explain how different they were in every single way; it would also explain her bitterness and sight disliking towards her. Her father would have told her if that was true, he wouldn't have kept something so huge from her. It was probably just because her mother was so embarrassed by the fact her husband had slept with another woman…or man. Come to think of it, she had never thought of the option that it could have been a man that her father slept with, which would explain her mother not liking the fact she only liked the same gender. It was possible, her father could be very eccentric at times and would even make comments about some men he saw, granted it was usually something along the lines of 'isn't he handsome Fay?' but she would notice the look in his eyes was a little different when he looked at a man than when he looked at her mother, however, this could have been due to the fact that they never got along. She would have to ask her mother, force her to give her some sort of answers. She knew her mother would be disappointed in her for eavesdropping on a private conversation but in her defence, they were talking quite loudly for the middle of the night and her mother owed her this, especially after how she had been treating her since Taeral died. She deserved answers, regardless of what they would be.

She trained for a while before calling it a day, telling everyone she was tired. In reality, she was going to find her mother, to get some answers. She went from room to room before finding her in the upstairs library. Her mother looked over at her from the armchair she sat in "looking for something?" she asked as Faylan walked towards her "I'm looking for answers" she replied as she sat opposite her. Her mother looked at her with a confused expression on her face. Faylan crossed her legs and looked at her mother with a stern look "I know"

"Know what?"

"I know what father did" she looked at her mother to try and see some sort of reaction but she was doing a good job of hiding what she was thinking and feeling. Her mother looked back at her "what do you know about it?"

"I know he had an affair and you both hid it from me" she crossed her arms, annoyed. She'd always hated people keeping secrets from her, she liked to know everything, maybe she was just nosey. Her mother sighed and set the book down that was in her hand, rubbing her face, preparing herself for what was probably going to be a very uncomfortable conversation "after we got married, your father and I started fighting, a lot, the stress of the crown and the aftermath of a war started to take its toll on us" she sighed "one night, I followed him, to find out where he was going…"she bowed her head, almost as if the memory of it hurt her "I found him with another woman" her voice wavered a little as she stood up, walking to the window and looking out, causing Faylan to turn around to face her "what's so awful about that?" Faylan asked "I mean, besides the fact he slept with someone else" she quickly amended and her mother scoffed and sighed "she was a lycan Fay" she took a deep breath "9 months later, you and your brother were left on our doorstep" she finished, looking at Faylan and hoping she understood what she was trying to tell her.

It eventually clicked in Faylan's brain and she gasped, a hand going to her mouth as she tried to process what this meant. She wasn't her mothers, it explained so much. At least her and her brother were still completely related but…she was half lycan. She was the child that Darion had told her about "that's why Taeral was killed wasn't it? That's the real reason, not whatever lies you fed people" she said, looking at her mother, standing up. Her mother turned to her "I couldn't let anyone know Fay, I had to keep it a secret" she pleaded, moving towards her. Faylan instinctively took a step back "no, no you wanted to hide your shame, fathers' shame and that's why you always treated me so badly, you hated what I represented, well, Taeral was the same as me, why was he never treated like I was?" she accused, crossing her arms angrily and her mother went silent, unable to answer her. Faylan just scoffed and left the room. Her mind was spinning as she headed to where they were keeping Darion, she needed to know what he knew about the child, what her destiny was.

~~~~~~~~

She told the guards to leave them when she got to the cell. After they had left, she looked at him. He was skinny and frail, his eyes sunken and he had bruises on his face and arms. His wrists were rubbed raw from where he'd tried to break free of the cuffs. He looked up at her when she entered "here to gloat? That you caught me" he asked, his voice weak and rough. She sat on the chair in front of him and took a sandwich out of her pocket "no, I'm just here to talk" she said gently and noticed his eyes light up when he saw the sandwich "give me the answers I want and you will get the sandwich, deal?" she said and he nodded eagerly "what do you want to know princess?"

"What do you know about the child? The half elf, half lycan child?" she asked, keeping her face expressionless so that he wouldn't figure out why she was asking him. He moved into a more comfortable position "not much, just what my father has told me, that this child will help to end the war and bring peace to our two species, the elves think the opposite though so they want to kill the child, we just want to save it and protect it so that it can bring peace" he said and she nodded along "so what happens if I find the child?"

"Take it to my father, it will be safest there" he said and he went to say something but then stopped, trying to read her expression before his eyes went a little wide "you know where the child is, don't you?" he leaned up on his knees, eagerly waiting for her response and she just nodded. He started to laugh "oh thank god, we need to get them to my father, you have to get me out of here" he said, his voice frantic and she handed him the sandwich "it might not be that easy" she said as he ate the sandwich "what do you mean?" he said, his voice muffled by the sandwich. She rested her hands on her knees "I don't know how I'd get you out of here and you're assuming I want to get you out"

"I can help you and the child, I can get them to safety and this war can be over, no one else needs to die" he replied once he'd finished eating. His voice was genuine and sincere and she wanted to trust him. She wanted to tell him the truth, she wanted to tell someone, anyone, about it. It was causing more questions than answers and she didn't know how to act anymore, she didn't even know who she was, not entirely. Her life had been based on a lie, a secret, that her father and mother had hid from her and her brother. Her brother had died not knowing the truth about who he was. She owed it to him to find out what they were.

Almost as if he could sense the internal crisis that she was having, Darion asked "are you alright princess?" he asked, tilting his head to the side, his voice soft. She sighed "I can't believe I'm about to tell you this but I suppose it is dire circumstances" she sighed and he leaned forward, listening to her "what is it?" he asked and she sighed "I found something out today and I think you might be the only one who won't look at me weirdly because of it or hate me for it" she said, she was surprised that she was being so honest to him, she barely knew the guy. He listened to her, letting her talk "my mother told me something about my father and me that has kind of got me having a little bit of a crisis" she half laughed as she stood up, pacing the room "my father had an affair on my mother before my brother and I were born and well…" she stopped and looked at him and he nodded "you weren't your mothers' children?" he offered and she nodded before continuing "the woman my father slept with…was a lycan" she said the last bit quietly, he was nodding along and then stopped once she stopped talking "you mean…"

"yeah" she said "I'm the child we were talking about finding and I didn't even know it" she sighed and sat back down in the chair "I don't even know who I am anymore" she put her head in her hands, feeling incredibly lost and confused. He moved towards her, as far as the chains would let him "I know who you are" he said "you're the thing we've been looking for, the person who can end all this bloodshed" he said, gently. She moved her hands away from her face "what the hell do I do now? I can't tell the others, they'll…"

"Kill you?" he said sympathetically "I know, it's a terrible situation but if you get me out of here, I promise to protect you" he said sincerely. She actually believed him when he said that. She nodded "okay well, how do we get you out? There are people everywhere and it won't take long for them to realise we are gone" she thought as she got up and started pacing the room again. He looked up at her "come back when everyone is asleep, there will be less people around and less chance of getting caught" he suggested and she nodded "okay, I'll get some supplies for us and come back at midnight, okay? Think you can hold out till then"

"Of course, it's only a few more hours" he nodded and moved back to his spot in the corner as she moved to the door "thank you" she said and he gave a single sharp nod and smiled at her and she left the room, bumping almost immediately "oh hi Nik" she said, trying to sound casual and he gave her a weird look "why were you talking to Darion?"

"Just to see if he had any information on his fathers' plans" she said, giving him a quick smile before starting to walk away. He grabbed her arm and pulled her into a nearby room "look, I heard you; okay? What you told him about your father" he said and she moved away from him "you were eavesdropping on me?"

"What? No! I was just the next person to talk to him but I came down early and they said you were in there so I listened in, trying to see if he'd tell you anything, so yes…I guess I was eavesdropping a bit" he rubbed the back of his neck awkwardly before snapping back to a look of betrayal and annoyance "how couldn't you have told me this?"

"I didn't know until an hour ago" she hissed, defensive that he would think she would keep it from him, of course he was right but she would have told him eventually. He crossed his arms and looked at her "you weren't planning on telling any of us, not even Eliana, how could you?!"

"Well, since you heard most of the conversation, you would have heard the bit where I said that you and the others would have me killed because of the belief that I would make everything worse" she snapped back, a little too loudly before sighing "I was going to tell you all, when it was safe" she explained but his expression didn't change "so you were just protecting yourself?" he accused and she opened her mouth to answer but shut it when she couldn't deny that he was telling the truth. He scoffed and walked out the door "Nikolas! Come on!" she called after him but she got no response "dammit!" she cursed, hitting the wall with her fist, putting a hole in it. She cursed in pain, pulling her hand back and seeing that she'd damaged her knuckles quite badly though in that moment, she didn't care. She had messed everything up with Nikolas, he probably hated her now and was telling everyone else about what she was. She needed to leave and soon.

She realised that she couldn't wait until tonight, she came up with a new plan. She made her way upstairs and packed a big bag full of clothes, food, weapons and a map before heading back down to the cell. The guards looked at her "my mother needs to talk to you about something, she didn't say what, I'll watch the prisoner" she said calmy and they gave her a strange look. She looked back "go,

don't want to keep the queen
waiting" she said and they hurried
away to find her mother. She
checked if the coast was clear
before opening the cell door and
racing over to Darion "we need to
go, quickly and quietly" she said as
she unlocked his cuffs "Nikolas
knows and I don't know how long
we have before I join you in this
cell so we need to go now" she said
and stood up, helping him up. He
looked at her "lead the way" he
said, rubbing his wrists. He
followed her out of the castle,
nearly getting caught a few times
before they made it outside. They
heard shouting and panic inside
"dammit, hurry!" she hissed quietly
and they ran into the forest,
leaving her home and her life
behind.

Chapter 18

They didn't stop until they were far enough away that all they could hear was the noises of the forest. Faylan stopped and leaned against a tree, out of breath and Darion crouched down a little, his hands on his knees, his rapid weight loss was clearly taking a toll as he swayed a little. She placed a hand on his shoulder "Rest a little, we'll be okay for a while"

"Have you got anything to eat in there?" he asked as he sat down. She handed him some food from the pack and a container of water "Here" she smiled and he took it, eating and drinking happily. She looked around, making sure nothing was sneaking up on them as he rested for a while "Where are we? I can mark out where we need to go if you have a map" he said once he'd finished eating, he already sounded a little healthier and she nodded, getting the map out the pack and a pencil. She put an X on the map where they were and handed it to him. He analysed the map for a few moments before marking out the fastest route to where they needed to go "We should be there in 2 days, my father will look after us" he said and she nodded "Well I have nothing to go back to so I hope you're right" she half-joked and he looked at her sadly "I'm sorry, what happened with Nikolas anyways?" he asked, looking at her. She launched into the story, trying to keep her voice steady as she told it, the emotions were still very raw. He stayed quiet as she spoke, his face a mixture of sadness and anger. He hated that Nikolas had reacted that way and he was sad that it had ended up with her having to leave "I know you may not trust me yet but I promise, I will never betray you and it's not just because of what you are" he said softly and she chuckled "thank you" she smiled at him and went silent for a moment, thinking about Eliana. She hadn't had time to leave a note or tell her anything, she probably hated her for abandoning her. She knew she would never forgive her and she honestly didn't blame her. Nikolas had probably told her what she was and she probably wanted nothing to do with her now. Nikolas had probably made her out to be a horrible person and she started to believe that she was one, the more she thought about it "I'm a terrible person; aren't I?"

"What makes you think that?" Darion asked, looking over at her. She came over and sat next to him "I'm half of the enemy, to my people at least, and the rest of the world and I didn't even know it until today"

"That's not your fault, you didn't know, your parents never told you and made it impossible to find out yourself," he said sincerely "If you're made out to be the villain by your own people, they're not the right people for you"

"I don't even know who my people are anymore," she said sadly. He gently patted her shoulder "Well, for now, you have me and once we get to my fathers, you'll have the lycans behind you as well" he smiled and her, and she nodded, maybe this wasn't going to be such an awful thing after all, maybe some real good could come out of her family's mess.

~~~~~~~~~~~

They spent the rest of the day walking; Darion was slightly ahead with the map. Faylan was too wrapped up in her own thoughts to care that they hadn't really spoken since they stopped the first time. He had given her a lot to think about. Maybe she wasn't the problem that she thought she was, maybe she could end the war and go home. She'd be welcomed home like a hero…she hoped. She already missed her home, Eliana, and Nikolas. She knew she couldn't go back until the war was over, whichever way it went. She wanted to be back in her bed, wrapped up in Eliana's arms while she read a book or simply slept. She held back the tears at the thought that she may never see her again depending on how the war went and what Nikolas had told her, he probably had told everyone and sent out parties to hunt her and Darion down and kill them.

She caught up with Darion after a while, when the sun started to set "Shall we stop for the night soon?" she suggested and he nodded "Yes, one more hour, and then we will" he smiled and she nodded, walking beside him for the remaining hour of their day. She helped to set up a small campfire and somewhere to sleep once they stopped for the night. She sat

down opposite him at the fire,
warming her hands over the fire
"What's he like? Your father" she
asked and he chuckled "he's pretty
cool, always let me do my own
things, let me learn from my own
mistakes" he said "though he was
harsh when he needed to be, he
set me straight when I needed it.
My mother was never around so he
had to take on both roles, she took
her own life when I was a child" he
said and she looked at him through
the fire, ignoring the burn in her
eyes from the brightness of the
flames "I'm so sorry" she said but
he waved her off "I don't
remember her and it was a very
long time ago, I've come to terms
with it" he said "she was unhappy
with her life and didn't want to live
anymore, nothing I can do about
that" he said. His views on the
topic of his mother were very
matter-of-fact, she didn't really see
any emotion behind his voice. He
was indifferent to it but she did

sense a bit of anger towards his mother because she left him. He cleared his throat "anyways, you'll like my father and I am sure he'll like you, though he is quite hard to please but he wants this war over just as much as we do, he'll be over the moon that you're real and not just some myth" he chuckled lightly and she smiled "I'm definitely real, last time I checked" she giggled "just have to keep you alive now" he said "we're still in your territory, we'll be safe once we make it to lycan territory. Let's just hope that no one finds us before then" he said and she nodded, suddenly becoming a little more paranoid that people were watching her from the trees, waiting to attack when they went to sleep "Can we take it in turns to keep watch?"

"Just what I was thinking, I'll take first watch, you get some rest" he smiled, taking a knife out of the pack as she lay down on the hard forest floor. She wasn't going to get much sleep on this floor she thought as she closed her eyes, listening to the wind rustling the trees, the owls hooting from their perches, and the crickets chirping from where they hid in the grass. It was incredibly loud but also very calming at the same time. She had always loved the sound of nighttime in the forest, it was so full of life and yet so quiet at the same time. She let her mind wander as she slowly fell into an uncomfortable and restless sleep.

~~~~~~~~~~

She was running through her home, guards on her tail when she tripped, falling down the stairs and landing in front of her father's throne "Thought you could run did you?" Nikolas's menacing voice came through the haze from where she had hit her head "We will always find you, no matter where you go" Eliana's voice came from the other side of her "You really thought I could love a mutt like you" she sneered and Faylan teared up "no, stop it, you're just being horrible"

"It's not horrible if it's the truth" she scoffed "I always preferred Nikolas, that's the real reason I kept you around" She took Nikolas's hand in hers as Faylan's mother walked over to her "What a disappointment" she snarled and brought a knife down towards her face.

Faylan woke with a loud gasp, her heart pounding and her breathing was uneven and ragged. She wiped the sweat from her brow and sighed, Darion looking over at her "You alright?" he asked gently and she nodded "Just a bad dream" she sighed, sitting up. Darion nodded "What was it about?"

"Just the usual anxieties," she said as she fixed her hair, tying it up into a ponytail and then finding herself something to eat "I can keep watch for a while if you want to sleep," she said, noticing that he was struggling a little to stay awake. He looked at her and nodded "I'd appreciate that" he smiled and made himself comfortable on the floor, almost immediately falling asleep. She looked at him for a moment before turning her gaze to the forest around them. The fire was almost completely out and she didn't want to risk lighting it again and drawing any unwanted attention.

She kept watch for the rest of the night, watching the sun rise over the trees. She loved watching the sky change from pitch black to beautiful colours of orange and red. She stared up at the sky for a long time, not noticing that Darion had woken up and had started making some food for them both. He walked over to her and handed it to her "Let's have some breakfast and then move on" he said and she nodded, eating her food. She was surprised that he had managed to make a decent breakfast out of their supplies. She listened to the forest wake up as she ate.

~~~~~~~~~~

They made it to Darion's home a day later. They were both tired and their bodies were stiff from sleeping on the hard ground. A few lycans met them at the gates, growling until they noticed Darion. They quickly opened the gate, letting him in and grabbing Faylan by her arms, holding her still "Let her go" he ordered "Now, before I tear your arms from your body" They instantly let go and he led her inside, the building was beautiful, it was made from stone and wood, there were big windows in the front which allowed a lot of sunlight in and also allowed them to see into the forest beyond them. There were plants along the base of the windows, drinking in all the sunlight they could. As she moved through the building, she realised it was much bigger than it seemed from the front, the gates and barricades had hidden the way the building actually looked, it was an old castle from the days when lycans were well respected. She noticed tall spires reaching up to the sky and there were winding staircases, and long verandas that looked out over the forest, some were high enough to see over the trees. As she walked beside Darion, she noticed that there was a room off to the side that was a floor-to-ceiling library and other rooms that were training rooms, kitchens, or dining rooms. Darion looked at her "You seem amazed?"

"Sorry, I just didn't realise that places like this still existed"

"This is one of the last of our castles that is still in almost perfect condition" he explained as he walked "My family and I are the only royalty left, well it's just my dad and me now," he said, opening a door at the end of the corridor "he can be a little cold, to begin with but as long as you're polite and can be of use to him, he'll like you," he said, Faylan feeling a slight surge of anxiety as she walked in beside him. Darion's father was a huge man, at least 6 foot 5, and with the body of an ox, he was incredibly well-built and intimidating. His piercing eyes stared down at her "D, who's this?" his voice was deep and gravely. Darion gave a short bow "Father, this is Faylan, she is an elf" he said and his father growled loudly "But she is also a lycan" Darion said quickly and his father looked at Faylan, analysing her "That is why I cannot place your scent, I smell elf and lycan but I assumed that was just my son"

"Her father, the king, had an affair with a lycan and she ended up having twins, her brother is dead but I believe she is the child we are looking for, the way we can end this war" Darion explained and his father nodded, moving towards her "what do you think?"

"I just want to stop the bloodshed," Faylan said quietly, looking up at him. Now he was closer she could see that his face was littered with burns and scars and he was blind in one eye. She was still very intimidated but she tried to act strong "I simply want to keep my family alive and I am sure you want the same"

"Of course, you can stay here, I am assuming you can't go home because of what you are," he said, she looked down at her boots and he nodded, sadly "I am sorry about that" he looked at his son "Darion, find her somewhere to sleep, I am sure she is exhausted" he said and she nodded and looked up at him "Thank you, sir" she said politely and he chuckled deeply "please, call me Cyran" he smiled and she nodded "thank you Cyran" she repeated and he gave her a nod "you're welcome, princess"

Darion led her up the grand, winding staircase and to a bedroom "Here we are, there is a bathroom attached so you will have complete privacy" he said and she smiled "Thank you, I really appreciate everything you've done for me" she said sincerely and he smiled "of course, seems I am starting to enjoy your company, so of course I will protect you" he chuckled lightly and left the room so she could rest. She sat down on the four-poster bed and looked around the room, the colour scheme was light green, coincidentally her favourite colour. She ran herself a bath and stripped down, getting in and allowing the warm water to relax her aching muscles and bones from the uncomfortable night's sleep. Her mind wandered back to her family, wondering what they were doing now, whether they were still planning to use their powers against the lycans, in which case she would need to warn Cyran and Darion.

She got out after a while and put on a nightgown she found in the chest by the bed, lying down under the covers. She fell into a deep and comfortable sleep.

Chapter 19

She woke up late the next day, feeling well-rested and more prepared to discuss their options and give them information that would help. She headed downstairs once she had gotten dressed and went to find Darion. She found him in the library, which she wasn't expecting, he hadn't given her the impression that he liked to read but there he was, his nose deep in a book with a cup of something hot beside him. He looked up when he heard footsteps "Hi, you sleep okay"

"Better than I have in a while" She nodded as she looked at all the books, it was almost overwhelming. He closed the book and looked at her "What's up?" he asked, clearly knowing that she wanted to talk to him. She walked over and sat on a chair opposite him "What do we plan to do exactly? With me" she asked, almost a little nervous for the answer. He chuckled "Nothing bad, if that's what you're worried about"

"That's reassuring" she chuckled "I just wanted to know what I'll be doing because I can fight, hand to hand, with a weapon and with my powers" she offered and he nodded "That will be useful, we haven't got a plan yet, that will need to be discussed with my father, he is the boss after all" he chuckled and Faylan smiled. She strangely felt at home with the lycans already, she felt important, valued, and accepted. She had that at home but not by everyone, with the lycans she felt like she had a proper purpose and not one that just spouted orders at people and helped to train elves who were completely useless when it came to using their powers even in the most basic ways. She also felt as though she was being treated as an equal to everyone else, she wasn't treated as anything but a normal elf, of course, she wasn't royalty amongst them, just a light at the end of the tunnel in the form of a girl.

She had a feeling that this wouldn't go the way that they wanted it to, it never did when it came to war. They wanted peace and she knew, deep down, beneath her hope that it may never happen and the bloodbath would continue until one species, or all of them, were extinct. She couldn't let that happen, not only to her family, Nikolas and Eliana but also to Darion and his father, she had come to respect and trust Darion and she didn't want to lose him. He had never asked her to do anything without making sure she was okay with it first and he was a true gentleman. She held back a chuckle as she thought 'My mother would approve of him'. Darion looked at her "Let's go talk to my father, I believe he has been doing some planning in the war room" he stood up and Faylan nodded, following him to the war room. It was just as elegant, if not more so, than the one in her parents' castle. There were maps everywhere and weapons mounted on the wall. She looked at them, one appeared to be a gun of some kind "It shoots silver" Cyran said when he saw her looking at it "It doesn't take normal bullets"

"How did you get it?" she asked, turning to face him "I took it from the witch that killed my daughter," he said in a cold tone. She looked at Darion, his sister was dead because of this war, no wonder he wanted it to end "I am so sorry for your loss" she said, completely understanding the feeling of losing a parent. Darion nodded "Thank you. I am sorry about your brother."

"Thank you," she said and moved towards the big table in the middle where Cyran was "What's the plan?"

"Right now? Negotiations, if that goes wrong then we will have to fight" Cyran said, looking at her "I don't want you to have to fight your own people, possibly your family…"

"If it must be done then I can prepare myself for it," she said, her voice sounding a little unsure. She didn't want to have to fight Nikolas, Eliana or even her mother but she needed this war to end. She wanted her old life back, her normal life. Cyran looked at her "I'll arrange a meeting if you'd feel comfortable attending with me?" he offered and she slowly nodded "Okay" she said "I won't need to say anything will I?" she asked, hoping that she wouldn't have to talk to the representatives as she wasn't sure what their reaction to her being there would be. Cyran moved to stand beside her and put a hand on her shoulder "Not if you don't want to" he said gently and she nodded, feeling a little more comforted with the notion that she wouldn't have to talk. She wouldn't even know what to say if she did have to.

~~~~~~~~~~~

She spent the rest of the day reading. She was woken up in the middle of the night by Darion, she'd fallen asleep in the chair "Sorry to wake you but they've agreed to the meeting" he said softly as she rubbed her eyes and yawned "Okay" She sighed and got up "I'll go and get ready"

"Okay, meet us in the war room" Darion smiled at her and she nodded and went upstairs to have a bath and get changed into something more appropriate for a meeting of this importance. She headed for the war room about an hour later, noticing a few elves, vampires, and witches in the main hall. She kept her head down as she walked past them but she heard them muttering to each other "That's her right?" one elf whispered "Yeah, that's the thing that betrayed us" another elf muttered back, hearing this, Darion cleared his throat and snarled, his fangs coming out and his eyes changing colour. The elves went silent and Faylan tried to hide her smile as she walked over to him "Thank you" she looked at him and he smiled "Of course, you ready princess?" he asked and she nodded and he guided her inside, his hand lightly pressed on her back. She looked around the room, noticing that it was her mother representing the elves, Nikolas the vampires, and Eliana representing the witches. The only one who made eye contact with her was her mother. Her mother gave her a slight smile and Faylan responded with a nod and moved to the corner, hopefully away from everyone's gaze. Darion sat beside her and the meeting started. Cyran made his proposal for peace before Nikolas interrupted "What makes you think we can believe you? Or her" he pointed accusingly at Faylan "She did lie to us after all"

"I have already explained the situation to you Nikolas" her mother snapped at him "Now listen to him and don't be rude," she said and he went quiet, allowing Cyran to continue "This bloodshed needs to end, we have all lost too much already" he said and looked at them all individually and Nikolas scoffed "we have lost because of you"

"We have all lost someone we care about" he kept going "and I don't want to lose anyone else"

"What could you have possibly lost that would make you understand" Nikolas scoffed and Cyran looked at him "My daughter," he said firmly and

Nikolas went quiet "Now, do we have a deal?"

"I am prepared to attempt peace," Faylan's mother said and Nikolas chuckled "Of course you would, your daughter is one of them"

"I am also an elf" Faylan spoke up, tired of his rudeness "Now stop being so damn rude and actually listen to what we are suggesting unless, of course, you'd like to keep fighting until no one is left?" she snarled, glaring at him and crossing her arms. He glared at her but went quiet. Darion let out a quiet snicker and his father looked at him and he mouthed 'sorry' and looked away. Cyran turned back to the others "Well?"

"I'd like peace, I don't want to lose any more of my people," Eliana said, glancing at Faylan, an unreadable look in her eyes before looking at Nikolas who looked and Cyran "As long as your men stop attacking my people, I will agree," he said "but I will not be associated with her"

"How many times do I have to tell you, I didn't know!" Faylan screamed at him and he looked at her in surprise "The real reason you hate me is because you don't know what I can do, you are just a scared little boy. You have no idea how hard the last few days have been for me! Oh yeah, I forgot, you don't care!" she screamed and stormed out, leaving Nikolas open-mouthed and Darion glared at him "some friend you are" he looked at Eliana "and you, you were meant to be her lover but somehow you can't defend her now?" he scoffed and followed Faylan out, leaving Eliana embarrassed.

Faylan ran to her room, standing out on the balcony. She took deep breaths to calm her anger, her hands shaking because of it. How dare he talk about her that way, what gave him the right? She didn't lie to him; she just didn't know what she was. If anything, she had more of a right to be angry because of how he reacted and how he acted today. She felt a presence behind her "You alright?" Darion said as he leaned on the railing beside her and she sighed "Yeah, just angry, he doesn't get to talk to me like that, not after everything we have been through"

"He just refuses to believe the truth for some reason, people can be like that sometimes and they just need a real smack in the face, which I'm pretty sure you gave him" he chuckled lightly and she cracked a smile "I hope I haven't messed everything up"

"Of course not, Nikolas will be put in his place and he'll fall in line if he doesn't want his people to continue to die" Darion reassured her. She sighed; he was right of course "I just hope he can let go of this anger for the sake of his people" She looked at Darion, who nodded "I hope so too, I don't like the way he spoke to you, how it's affecting you" she stammered, trying to argue and he chuckled "I'm very perceptive" he joked "do you want to come and say goodbye to your mother?"

"I suppose I should, shouldn't I" Faylan sighed "She did defend me today after all." Darion nodded and they went downstairs to the main entrance. She completely ignored Nikolas when she saw him and went over to her mother "Thank you, for defending me"

"Of course, you're my daughter sweetheart," she said, kindly, something Faylan was not used to "When are you coming home?"

"When it's safe" Faylan responded, shooting Nikolas a quick look "I am sure it will be before you know it" She smiled a little at her mother, who pulled her in for a hug "Your father would be so proud of you" she said quietly and Faylan hugged back when she heard this "thank you" she let go after a moment and her mother walked out the building, her guards following her.

Faylan turned and faced Nikolas as he walked over to her. She crossed her arms when he opened his mouth to say something and he quickly closed his mouth, seeing the look of anger and hurt on her face. He just walked past her, the vampire guards following him. She watched him go, her heart hurting a little because of how much all of this had cost her. She didn't know who she was anymore and she didn't even have her best friend to help her figure it out. She felt so lost and confused and she hated him for abandoning her and being awful to her for something she couldn't control and that she didn't know until a few moments before he found out. He didn't let her explain why she went to Darion to ask about this, he just got angry at her and stormed out. She sighed and looked at Eliana as she walked over to her. Her facial expression was unreadable. She looked at Faylan and gave her a small smile "How are you doing?" she asked, genuinely concerned about her and Faylan looked at her boots "I'm figuring it all out...I think" she replied, unsure. Eliana placed a hand on her shoulder "I am sure you will figure it out" she took a deep breath "But I can't be around while you do" Faylan's head snapped up when she heard this "What? Why?"

"I know you didn't know about this before the day you left but you didn't come to me, you went to a total stranger," she said "I thought you trusted me enough to talk to me about things, I thought you would come to me but I had to find out through Nikolas"

"I was going to tell you; I just knew it wouldn't be safe" Faylan sighed "I knew exactly how it would have ended for me and for anyone else who knew"

"What? We would have been killed?" Eliana said, in a slightly joking tone but stopped smiling when she saw the serious look on Faylan's face. She sighed "I would have protected you, us," she said "I don't think I can trust that you will tell me the truth anymore and I wish you all the best and I will be here for you but I cannot be with you, romantically," Eliana said and Faylan started to tear up and started to walk away, unable to continue the conversation, leaving Eliana in the empty hallway.

~~~~~~~~~~~~

She stayed in her room for the next few days, trying to process the conversation she had with Eliana, crying and barely eating, even though Darion brought her food. Darion sat on a chair next to the bed and looked at her "Want to talk about it?" he asked gently and she shook her head, tearing up again. He sighed and moved to sit on the bed, instinctively wrapping his arms around her "It'll be okay, I promise, it just takes time" he said reassuringly as she cried into his shoulder, holding onto him tightly. They stayed that way for a while before she moved away, sitting up and wiping her eyes and sighing. She was so fed up with crying and feeling numb, that it felt as though the universe was against her with the amount of hurt, she had experienced in the last few months. She had had enough, she just wanted to feel happy and safe again, to know who she was, and to have her old life back. She wanted her father, she knew he would know how to make her feel better, to make everything okay. Darion was helping though, even when he was just bringing her food, his presence just radiated safety and calm. She knew, even though she hadn't known him for very long, that he would be there for her and he wouldn't leave her and that wasn't just because of what she was.

She looked at him "What abilities do I have? As a half lycan?" she asked him. He looked at her a little surprised and moved so he was facing her completely "Well, when you learn how to turn, you'll be a complete wolf and when out of that state, you'll have enhanced hearing, sight, smell, strength and you'll have claws" he said, showing her his claws before looking at her "why do you ask?"

"Well, I have magic as an elf and I wondered if I would still have that"

"Yes, you will, if anything, you're more dangerous than a simple elf or lycan, no one will mess with you when you're fully trained if you want to be" he offered and she nodded "I want to be, it will give me something else to think of" he nodded as he listened and smiled "well, we'll see what happens at the next full moon and go from there with your training"

"Why?"

"We'll see how you handle your first turn first" he looked at her and chuckled "I know it's weird but that side of you was dormant so you never turned as your brain was tricked into believing you were just an elf and now you know and want it to come out, you'll turn tomorrow night at the full moon" he explained and she nodded, understanding. She just had to wait till tomorrow. She could do some physical training in the meantime. She looked at Darion "this might be a bit weird but would you stay with me tonight? I don't really want to sleep alone" she asked and he smiled and nodded "Sure, I'll stay in the chair if that makes you more comfortable" he suggested and she nodded "Okay" she smiled a little and he smiled back "do you want to come downstairs to have dinner? Or do you want to have it in here?"

"Let's go down, I can't stay in here forever, my body is stiff anyways so I need to move around" She chuckled a little and he smiled "All alright then" he chuckled and helped her up, both of them making a surprised face at each other when her joints clicked loudly as she moved her legs and arms. They both laughed softly "you weren't joking" Darion chuckled and Faylan giggled and clicked the joints in her fingers and cracked her neck, sighing in relief "that feels better"

"That sounds painful" Darion made a face "Sounds like you're breaking your neck," he said, making her chuckle and gently punch his shoulder "Come on, let's go have something to eat" she chuckled and walked downstairs.

Chapter 20

Faylan turned the next night. The pain was unlike anything she had ever felt. She felt each of her bones breaking and her teeth shifting to fit the fangs and her fingernails and toenails being pushed out by the claws. She started off screaming in agony and ended up howling by the end of it. Darion was by her side the entire time, trying to keep her calm and distract her from the pain. He turned after she did, to keep her company as he wasn't tied to changing at the full moon anymore, after a lycan turns the first few times, they are no longer tied to the moon cycle.

They spent the entire night running around the woods and even hunting a couple of animals. Once they turned back in the morning, they were both exhausted. Faylan made her way to her room and collapsed into bed, not caring that she was caked in dirt, leaves and spots of blood.

She woke up late in the afternoon, cleaning herself up and going to find Darion. She felt different, she felt stronger and more alive than she had ever felt. She felt ready to take on the world, though that could have just been the adrenaline from the night before. She found him in the kitchen, making something to eat. She didn't know he could cook, she always just assumed that someone else did it for him. He was humming softly to himself, his hair tied up in a slight bun, since she'd known him, his hair had grown a lot, a lot more than normal but maybe that was a wolf thing. She cleared her throat "Hi Faylan" he said, turning round to face her "I thought it was you, you hungry?"

"Starving" she chuckled and popped herself up on the counter "last night was insane" she said and he chuckled "it always is the first time it happens, I think the adrenaline lasted a week for me when I first turned, I felt on top of the world" he said as he cooked "once it wore off though, it did get a little overwhelming, being able to see, hear and smell everything was a huge sensory overload" he glanced at her "just something to look forward to" he joked and finished cooking after a few moments and plated the food for them both, placing the plated on the table. She hopped off the counter and sat at the table "I don't think I have ever felt more alive than I did last night" she said "it definitely took my mind off everything"

"Good" Darion smiled "I can't have you moping all the time, we got to have you living life and enjoying it right? I mean, the war is over" he smiled and she chuckled "let's not jinx it" she said and started to eat. She finished a few moments later and looked at him "so what happens now?"

"Well, we see if your magic still works and then we work on controlling your senses, that way it won't be so awful when the adrenaline wears off, I'd rather not have you live through what I did, it was awful" he said, shivering a little at the memory, as if his body remembered it involuntarily. She gently patted his shoulder "I appreciate that" she smiled lightly at him, making him smile back. She looked at him for a moment, she couldn't quite place the feelings she felt towards him, of course she was grateful for everything he had done for her and she would consider him a friend but there was something else, something below the surface that she didn't understand. She knew for a fact that she liked girls but she didn't know if she liked guys, she'd never experienced it before, aside from almost being forced into a marriage with Nikolas. She had been so wrapped up in her own world all her life that she never gave herself a chance to experience anything until Eliana. She was her first love and she knew she may never completely get over it but she wanted to be able to live her life, Eliana had made it clear that it was over. She needed to move on with her life, she wasn't coming back and she needed to understand that and find someone who wasn't going to leave, regardless of what came out about her or her family. She looked away, worried that she looked as though she was staring. Darion looked at her "everything ok princess?"

"Yeah, got lost in thought, nothing interesting" she said quickly and he chuckled "well okay then" he cleared up the table once they finished eating and walked with her back up to her room "you want to work on controlling your senses now?" he asked and she nodded. He sat cross-legged on her bed and the training began.

~~~~~~~~~~~~~

They worked on controlling her senses over the next few weeks. It was an amazing experience, each sense they worked on had a different effect on her. Her hearing was the most overwhelming experience, she could hear everything at once and everyone's conversations. Darion noticed she was overwhelmed and gently took one of her hands and spoke to her gently, getting her to focus on his voice. After a moment it calmed down and she sighed in relief. Her sense of smell and sight were a little easier to focus, they were less overwhelming and more interesting as she could see further and better in darkness and she could smell everything, she had never realised that Darion smelt like sandalwood and the forest, it was a really nice smell. She smiled, wishing she could bottle it, she had always adored the smell of the forest and to have a person constantly smell like that was amazing.

Faylan worked on her strength after that, she found it very funny that she was supposed to be super strong, she was a tall and skinny elf, it didn't look right to her. She was incredibly strong, Darion had her demonstrate on boulders in the nearby woods. She gasped in surprise and jumped back a little when she punched it and it split in half. Darion chuckled "cool huh?"

"Incredibly cool" Faylan giggled and they worked on controlling her strength so that she wouldn't accidentally hurt someone if they angered her but kept it so that she could really hurt someone in a fight. She collapsed into bed each night, exhausted but feeling on top of the world.

Darion and Faylan were sat in the library, taking a break from training for a day. Faylan had her nose deep in a book and Darion was drawing, curled up in an armchair in the corner. They stayed this way for hours before Cyran walked in and they both looked at him. He had an unreadable look on his face when he said "I need to talk to Faylan…in private" he added then end bit when Dario didn't move.

He got up and left the room before Cyran came and sat next to Faylan "what's going on?" she asked, confused. He took a moment to think before he said "it's your mother…she…"

"She what?" Faylan said, looking at him, now worried about what he was going to say. He sighed "she was killed"

"By who?" she asked, trying not to sound as angry as she felt "by a vampire" Cyran sighed "I believe it was because she agreed to peace with us and they didn't agree with it" he sighed and she clenched her fists "I need to find who did it"

"Maybe we should talk to Nikolas first?"

"He might have been behind it" she sighed "he does hate me after all and didn't want peace with me" she said and Cyran sighed, she was right after all "okay but let's try and do this calmly? We don't want to start a war just weeks after we ended one"

"Clearly someone didn't get that" she said angrily and Cyran gently put a hand on her shoulder, comfortingly before getting up and walking out of the room, talking to Darion about what was going on. She flung the book down that she was holding, aggressively and sighed. It was official, she had no family left. She needed revenge. Her mother did not deserve the fate that she got. In that moment, she didn't care about the peace, her mother had been murdered, she wanted justice for what happened. She needed it. Darion came back in a few moments later and looked at her, noticing the look on her face "so, what do we do first?" he asked, completely understanding the anger she felt, the want for justice. Faylan looked at him and gave him a smile, grateful that he didn't ask how she was or try to stop her going out and seeking justice. She knew that this might not end well for them, they could start another war but she needed justice and at least she had Darion helping her "let's get started" she said and they walked out the room together, starting the hunt for answers.

Printed in Great Britain
by Amazon